New Beginnings in Summit County

New Beginnings in Summit County

Summit County Series Book 3

Katherine Karrol

Contents

Chapter 1

From: info@GenealogyWeb.com

Subject: You have a DNA Match!

Dear Rick,

The DNA profile we have on file for you has been matched with another user. Our exclusive matching algorithm has calculated enough shared DNA to indicate a parent-child relationship.

To view the results and contact the user you have been matched with confidentially, click the link below. Your name will not be shown to the user you have been matched with until you give permission to do so.

"I have a child?"

Rick Weston had been lying in bed in his hotel room staring at the email for what seemed like an eternity. He couldn't move. He couldn't breathe.

"I have a child?"

He walked into the bathroom, splashed cold water on his face, and looked into the mirror.

This can't be real.

He picked his phone back up. As he looked at the email again, he half expected it to vanish. It was still there in black and white.

"How could this happen?" *You know how this happened, man.*

"Well, Lord, I suppose it's fitting that if You were going to give me a miracle child, it would be in the wee hours of Christmas morning."

∞∞∞

I have a child.

Those words were the first thought in his mind every time he woke up, which was often. He'd tossed and turned all night and didn't feel like he'd gotten any sleep.

He had grabbed his phone and re-read the email several times during the night as he tried to make sense of the news. He'd thought about old girlfriends who could be the mother and made several drafts of letters to send to the mystery child.

The list of potential mothers of the child was easy because it was very short. He was never very religious until a few years ago, but he always considered himself a decent, moral person and never slept around. The only women he had been with were women he was in committed relationships with, and all but one of his relationships had lasted at least a couple of years. He had also taken a break from women for a few years after getting his heart blown to bits when he was a new Air Force pilot.

Glad he didn't have the history with women that some of his buddies there had, he shook his head picturing a couple of them trying to remember all the women they'd been with. The humor break only lasted a moment and he once again returned to the gravity of the situation.

He pictured his teenage nephew and niece who he had always been so close to and wondered about his child. "Do I have a son? A daughter? Is there a boy out there who's grown up without a father figure to show him how to be a good man? Is there a girl who thinks her dad doesn't love her and thinks all men are jerks because of it? Lord, You've got to help me with this one. Someone out there probably thinks their dad doesn't give a rip. Maybe they don't even know I exist. Maybe they call someone else 'Dad'. How could this be?"

He opened his notepad app for the twentieth time.

"Hi, son or daughter, I'm your dad."

Delete.

"Hi, I don't know who you are or who your mother is, but I sure hope to meet you someday."

Delete.

"Hi. I wonder if you were as surprised to get a notification of a match as I was. That notification was the first hint that I've ever gotten that I'm a father."

Close, but no cigar.

He groaned. "This would be more satisfying if I was writing this on paper so I could crumple it up and whip it against the wall. I need words. What on earth do you say to a child who probably thinks you abandoned them?"

Chapter 2

F aith Stevens looked at the clock. Again. Time ticked slowly as she waited in line for the phone on her unit. Her roommate approached, smiling with two cups of Bulletproof Coffee. "Christmas coffee delivery for you, Faith — I thought you would like to enjoy it while you talk to your daughter."

"Thanks, Brandy. I'm so glad it was your turn to make the coffee today so I could get in the phone line. I just don't want to miss the chance to wish Rachel Merry Christmas *on* Christmas and don't know if she has plans that will take her out of the house today."

"I know. I'll be doing the same thing in a few hours when it's time for me to make my calls. Our days of being too depressed to call our kids on holidays are over. Just think, next year we won't be calling our kids – we'll be celebrating *with* them again."

"That's going to be wonderful. All of us here have missed out on too much with our families. Here's to this being the last time we miss out on anything with the people we love." She held up her coffee mug to toast Brandy and smiled.

This Christmas was a day of hope. The past several years were a painful blur to Faith, and she prayed for months that God would pave the way for her to start over. A Christmas phone call would be part of her new start.

It was always somewhat awkward to call Rachel, and she felt the familiar knot in her stomach when it was finally her turn and she dialed the number. Their relationship had been loving but distant for years and if someone listened in on their calls, they would think that Rachel was the mother and Faith the wayward daughter.

They had talked the week before and Faith had finally told her where she was. It was a relief to finally tell her and the conversation had gone better than usual. It was strange but freeing to be completely honest with her, and Faith hoped this conversation would go as well.

Rachel picked up on the third ring. "Merry Christmas, Sweetheart. It's Mom."

"Mom! Merry Christmas. I'm surprised— glad to hear from you again so soon. Is everything ok?"

Faith cringed. *A week is 'so soon' and surprising for a mother and daughter to talk. I've got a lot of repairs to do on this relationship.*

"Everything is ok. I just wanted to talk to you today to wish you a Merry Christmas and didn't know if you and Grandma had plans. How are you celebrating today?"

"We're going over to Auntie Ev's in a little while and later going to have Christmas dinner with the Coopers." *The Coopers, as in the ex-boyfriend's family? I have missed a lot.*

"The Coopers? Derek's family?"

"Yes, we— Derek and I are back together. We got engaged last night."

She could hear the discomfort in her daughter's voice. *She shouldn't feel bad about having big life events that I'm not part of. And I hate not being a part of them.*

"Wow, Rachel, congratulations! No wonder your voice sounded so happy when you picked up the phone. When is the wedding?"

"How are you doing, Mom? Are you still at the place you told me about?"

She sounds scared – the way she always sounds when she asks if I'm ok and where I'm living. She also completely dodged my question.

"I'm good. And yes, I'm still in the treatment center in Kentucky. We've been making preparations all week so that we can have a special Christmas today." *Even though we are all away from our families.*

Rachel sounded relieved. "That's good. I'm glad you get to celebrate Christmas. I didn't know how they did things there."

"I know I didn't tell you much about the program, but it's a Christian place and they have Bible studies and prayer groups available along with all the other physical treatments and psychotherapy groups. Needless to say, we're having a special Christmas celebration today."

When she noticed the line waiting for the phone, she was reminded that time was short. "I'm hoping I can tell you all about it sometime soon, but since I can only talk for a few minutes, I want to talk about *you*. I'm so happy you and Derek found your way back together. I don't know what happened between you so long ago, but I remember how devastated you were when you broke up." It pained her to remember all the missed opportunities. "I'm sorry I wasn't there for you through that, Rachel. I'm sorry for a lot of things, and I hope to make them up to you now that I'm back on my feet."

"I know, Mom. You don't have to make up for anything. I just want to see you get better. You sound really good. You said when we talked that they're helping with the pain and the—and other stuff there?"

"You can say it, Sweetheart — the addiction. Yes, they're helping with both here and I feel better than I've felt in years. I feel like myself again now that the pain is better and I've been completely off pain meds for five months. I can honestly say that I feel better every day." She paused, giving herself a moment to swallow down the tears that were threatening. "I've got less than six weeks to go until I've completed the full year."

"Wow, Mom, that's great! I'm really proud of you."

Proud. No stopping the tears now.

"Thank you, Sweetheart." She pushed to get the words out and keep her voice strong. She hated crying and refused to do it in front of Rachel. "Merry Christmas and please give Grandma a hug for me, okay?"

"Okay, Mom. Merry Christmas. I'm glad we got to talk *on* Christmas this time. I love you."

As she hung up the phone, she couldn't stop the tears.

She's proud of me. Proud of me.

I'll bet she never thought she would say those words. I started believing I would never earn those words. Thank You, Lord, for making this possible.

Chapter 3

R ick sat staring at the blank screen again. *Just write something and hit send.* He started typing and hoped for the best.

Hello. I've started this letter 50 times and can't come up with the perfect words to say to you, so I'm just going to say something and hit send. Please forgive me if it's terrible.

My name is Rick and I received an email several hours ago saying there was a parent-child match through the genealogy database. It was both the most unexpected and the best Christmas present I ever could have hoped to receive. I've spent the last hours writing and rewriting this message and trying to figure out how I could not have known about you. I just pray that you haven't gone your whole life thinking that I knew and didn't care. I'm so sorry. I hope you want to talk to me as much as I want to talk to you.

I've included my contact information below and you can call me any time, day or night. Or if you would rather give me your number, I will call you. I know this information is probably shocking to you too, so I understand if you need time.

He clicked *Send* before he chickened out.

∞∞∞

Please tell me more about yourself. I'd like to know more about you before I say much. For starters, why didn't you know you had a child?

Wow, he or she gets right to the point.

Thank you for writing back so soon. I wasn't sure if you would want to talk to me. I'm not sure how to answer that question because I'm asking it myself, but I'll give it a shot.

I've never been married but have been in a few long-term relationships. I have never been the kind of guy who got around or had one-night stands, and I have never been told by any woman I've been involved with that I was the father of a child, so I'm at a bit of a loss here.

When I saw the notification about this match, I planned to contact my former girlfriends, but wanted to contact you directly first, or at least try to. It kills me that I didn't know about you. I swear to you that I would have been there for you and would have tried to be the best dad I could have been if I had known. I always wanted to be a dad and thought I would be one, but God had His own plans for me.

As I said, I haven't been married, and before this morning, I thought I had never had kids. I'm a commercial pilot and travel all over the world for work, but I'm based in Chicago. I have parents, a sister and brother-in-law, and a niece and nephew who live near Grand Rapids (MI, if you're not familiar) and I visit them regularly. Working, time with family, church, and online classes take up most of my time.

I hope we can get to know each other. Because of my job, I can travel anywhere I want to go and my schedule is flexible. I'd like to come and meet you sometime if you ever decide you want to meet me, even if just for lunch.

Good enough for now. Don't overwhelm the kid.

He clicked *Send* and said a prayer that it would be well received.

Chapter 4

"This turned out to be a nice Christmas, huh?" Faith and Brandy drank chamomile tea as they talked about their day, as was their nightly ritual.

"Christmas has been the 'I'm missing out on everything' holiday for so long and I spent so many years with my back turned to Jesus." She shook her head. "It was great to actually celebrate His birth and to talk to Rachel. My greatest gift is getting the two most important relationships in my life back on track. Spending the day with everyone here was wonderful, too — it was great to play games and sing carols instead of crying and sleeping. It's time to put *that* Christmas tradition to rest for good." She chuckled.

Brandy laughed too. "Definitely. I haven't had the chance to ask you with everything going on here today, but how did your phone call with Rachel go?"

"It was more emotional than I expected, to be honest. It was great to get to talk to her, of course. She got engaged last night and I didn't even know that she and her ex-boyfriend were back together." She took a breath, firm in the decision she made after hanging up the phone. "You know how I've been going back and forth about where I'm going to settle when I leave here — I want to go home. The biggest part of taking my life back is getting a better relationship with her. We've barely spent any time together over the last several years and I don't want to lose more. I want to go home and be a part of her life while I rebuild mine."

Brandy smiled at her. "You're ready for it. I'm sure she will be thrilled."

Faith was thankful that she and Brandy had been put together in a room. She was a great person and had such a similar history with an injury that changed the course of her life that it was easy to talk to her about the rest of the collateral damage after such an event.

She was going to miss the people and the safety of Healing Rock — she had learned to cope well within these walls. It would be very different when she left, but she felt more ready to face challenges than she had in years. *Funny how different life is when you're not hooked on painkillers or in terrible pain constantly. Funny how different life is when you have hope.*

It had been a long road to get to this point. When she heard about the program at Healing Rock, she felt like it was her last chance. She was depressed, hopeless, and living in a fog of pain, narcotics, and heartbreak.

She was several months into the program before she even let herself hope that she might have success. Her longest stint in rehab to date had been forty-five days, so she didn't have much trust in treatment *or* herself by that time. Now that she was only weeks away from completing the strenuous and compre-hensive program, she needed to make some decisions and plans for what was next.

Up until the phone call with Rachel, she hadn't decided where she was going to go when she was discharged. There was an op-tion of a transitional living home, but for the first time since her life fell apart twenty-three years before, she not only *wanted* to go home, but felt ready to do so.

She had refused to move there for all those years, preferring to struggle on her own than have to be a drain on her mother and daughter or be pitied by people she had known her whole life. Now that she was feeling better physically, free of addiction, and feeling like herself, she *wanted* to start over in her hometown.

She just didn't know if her mother or her daughter would want her there.

Chapter 5

R ick had another fitful night. He was thankful that he had a good First Officer on the trip from Berlin to Chicago. He was going to be taking full advantage of the chance for a nap during the flight. The likelihood of sleeping for more than an hour was slim, but after the past two nights, an hour sounded great.

The excitement and romanticism of international flights had long since worn off, and he had been contemplating his future and long-term plans for months. Receiving the news about having a child put everything into a different light. If he had the chance to get to know this son or daughter, he was taking it. Maybe his plans to either change to a different flight schedule or retire from the airline and buy a charter plane might need to be put on a faster timetable.

Slow down. You don't even know if he or she is going to want to meet.

He was glad that he lived in a time with smartphones and in-flight Wi-Fi. The ten-hour flight over the Atlantic Ocean would have been pure torture if he wasn't able to check his email — not that checking it every few minutes wasn't torturous. He hoped the mystery child would write back soon, but he hadn't heard anything. *It's only been twenty-four hours. Give it time.*

"Lord, I hope I didn't scare him or her off with my response.

Did I move too quickly when I asked for a visit? My gosh, this is worse than dating."

$$\infty\infty\infty$$

The next email arrived and Rick sighed in relief.

How long has your longest relationship with a woman been? What is your longest friendship? Would your niece and nephew vouch for your character? What would they say about you? You mentioned God and His plans. What is your relationship with Him?

Again, right to the point. Sounds like a therapist or attorney, even though they couldn't possibly be old enough. Okay, I'll bite.

My longest dating relationship was six years, with a woman who was also a pilot for the airline I work for. The friends I'm closest to are ones who I've gotten to know over the past three years since I've been involved in my church. I have several friends who I've known for much longer, but we're not as close now since I changed my lifestyle.

Ugh, I hope this doesn't sound like I turned into a holier-than-thou churchy person who got religion and dumped their 'sinner' friends.

I still see those friends at work and have a good relationship with them, but I just don't drink with them any more on work trips. When I have downtime, I'm usually visiting with my family in Michigan or working on my master's degree.

My relationship with God is the most important relationship in my life. He turned my life around at a time when I needed it. He brought me to Himself, got me sober, and gave me some great friends and a new direction and purpose in life.

My niece and nephew would say that they talk to and text with me regularly and that I have been to every play and game that I've been able to get to. They would say that I'm a decent guy, caring, fun, and that I'm more adventurous than the two of them put together, as evidenced by the fact that I'm answering these questions and willing to answer as many as I need to.

I'm happy to stay in the hot seat, but I'm curious about you, too. I don't even know your gender or age, let alone your name.

And if I know your age, I'll know who your mother is. What an embarrassing thought. I never thought I would be the guy who would find out he had a kid and have to figure out who the mother was.

He thought back to the possibilities. The only former girlfriend he could count out was Trina, the pilot and the longest-term girlfriend. It had only been four years since they had broken up and unless the child was a prodigy, he or she would not be having the kind of conversations he had been having through the emails so far.

"Lord, please let them tell me *something* so I can know what I'm dealing with here."

∞∞∞

Bzzz.

The child you're matched with is a twenty-five-year-old woman. I am not her. She is my best friend and is one of the most wonderful people on this earth. When she submitted the DNA, she gave access to myself and to her other best friend but did not sign into the database herself. She asked us to be her gatekeepers of information in case anything of significance came through.

We would like to speak with you on the phone before we pass anything about this match on to her. I've attached several times that we are both available for a conference call with you below. Please let us know when it will be most convenient for you."

I'm not sure if I'm most glad that my daughter is not this bossy or that she has friends that are this protective.

My daughter. Wow. My daughter. I have a daughter. A twenty-five year old daughter.

Twenty-five years old means that twenty-six years ago—

Faith! He gasped and felt like his heart stopped.

The One Who Got Away got away with my daughter.

Chapter 6

Faith was glad to have the therapy groups back the day after Christmas. She had been doing a lot of thinking and praying since her conversation with Rachel on Christmas morning and was ready to process.

"Who wants to start us off today?"

Faith looked around the group. Everyone was either looking at the floor or at each other. "I'll start if no one else wants to. I spoke to my daughter yesterday morning and she told me that she's engaged. I had been unsure about where to go when I leave here, and I decided that I definitely want to go home to Michigan." It was surprising how good it felt to say it. "I'm not sure if my daughter or my mother would really want me to go back to Hideaway — the town they live in — but Summit County is big enough that I could move close without it being too much for them. I've missed so much of my daughter's life that I can't imagine missing more. I need the group to help me get ready to go home."

"What do you think you need to do to be ready?"

"I need to get myself ready to talk with them, for one, and see how they feel about the idea. They don't know the growth I've had since I've been here because I haven't shared it with them. I realized I was a little afraid the spell would be broken if I did, but God showed me last night as I was praying that there is no spell. I've been growing and healing, and I'm not the same person who came here almost a year ago. I'm better physically and I'm not on narcotics. I'm not breaking spells or jinxing anything just because I say it out loud."

She chuckled and the group chuckled with her — they knew the struggle.

"I need to be ready to hear them say that they don't want me to be there and to accept it if that's what happens. I also need to apologize for what I've put them through and to show them that I'm strong again, that I'm *me* again. Rachel doesn't even know the real me. She's only known the depressed, anxious, struggling mom who was always in pain and always on drugs. The mom she knew was weak and unstable. It's time for her to know the real me."

Brandy smiled at Faith as she spoke. "Good for you, Faith. I think it's great that you want to go home. You're not even the same person you were two weeks ago, let alone when I got here six months and four days ago. I don't know how I would have made it this far if it wasn't for your help and encouragement."

I'm going home.

Chapter 7

Rick looked at the clock. Fve minutes had passed since his last glance. So far, he had gone to the gym *and* for a run, vacuumed, cleaned out behind his refrigerator, and organized his bookshelf.

He was glad to be back home for a few days and glad for the regular routine to fall into while he waited. The past couple of days had seemed like an eternity as he waited for the 'appointment' with The Gatekeepers.

His friend Tim had come over and prayed with him, and now he just needed to pass another twenty minutes before the call. He hadn't been as nervous going into combat as he was getting ready for this conversation. These women would determine if he could make contact with his daughter.

Tim had suggested that he keep his answers brief with them. He needed to show them that he was a good guy so they would let him talk to their friend, but details and private information should be saved for his daughter.

What had Faith told her about him? He still didn't know why she had left him and broken his heart so long ago. He wondered if she had found someone else and if that man had the privilege of being called Dad by his daughter.

There were so many unanswered questions that he had no

idea what he was walking into. He hated not knowing what kind of situation he was in. The carefully ordered life he had built felt like it was all thrown into a tumbler and shaken.

"Lord, I'm trying to hand this over to you. Please help me to answer their questions well and to make a good impression on them. Please make it so I can meet my daughter."

He tried to picture her. She wasn't a little girl. She was a grown woman who could even be a mother herself. He wasn't quite ready to picture himself as a grandfather, but realized he had to be ready for that possibility too. He wondered if she looked like Faith, with those honey brown eyes that he used to get lost in.

He remembered the first time they met. He and a buddy who was also preparing to go into the military after graduation had gone out for pizza to celebrate the end of the semester and she was their waitress. His buddy thought of himself as a smooth talker and pulled out all of his best flirting tricks on her, but she shot down every line he tried. He even pulled the I'm-going-to-a-war-zone-soon line, but she wasn't falling for it.

Rick was so embarrassed by his friend, and taken with her, that he emptied his pockets of all the money he had for groceries for the next week and left it as a tip, along with an apology written on a napkin. He started living on ramen noodles and popcorn so he could go for pizza more often and eventually got her to go out with him, once he showed her that he was nothing like his friend.

As he was lost in the memory, the phone rang.

"Hello, this is Rick." Trying to sound casual while feeling like he had a mouth full of sand and a truck on his chest was not easy.

"Hello, Rick. This is Brianna."

"And this is Shelby."

The Gatekeepers had names.

"Hello, Brianna and Shelby. Thank you for being willing to talk to me. I assume you both have more questions."

"Yes, we do. The biggest question is, what are you hoping to gain from talking to her?" *Right to the point again.*

"You must be the one I've been emailing with."

The other one let out a giggle, then spoke. "Please excuse Brianna. She's the blunt one. I'm the nice one, so you can direct your answer to me if you prefer."

"To be honest, I'm glad my daughter has friends who are so protective of her. I never got the chance to be protective, and I'm glad God sent the two of you to be in her life when I couldn't." His words lodged in his throat and he took a swig of water.

Brianna broke the silence. "I prefer to think I'm direct. I just want to know where you've been all these years and what your intentions are now. Did you really not know?"

"I really didn't know. Faith never told me she was pregnant. If she had, I would have tried harder to get her to marry me and things would be very different now. All I want is the chance to get to know my daughter and try to make up for twenty-five years of not being there for her." He felt like there was a vice grip on his throat and couldn't go on.

"So you know that Faith is her mother. We'll take that as a good sign." Shelby really was the nicer of the two.

"Sorry to be so hard on you. You seem like a decent guy, but we can't be too careful when we're protecting our best friend." Okay, Brianna wasn't so bad, either.

"I get that, and I really do appreciate it. You don't know anything about me and you don't want your friend hurt by some jerk coming in and wanting to play Daddy or not caring about her feelings. Does she think I abandoned her?" His voice broke.

"You can ask her that when you talk to her."

Chapter 8

Faith gathered up her courage and dialed the number. She had prepared herself for every possible outcome of this conversation and was ready for whatever answer she got.

"Good morning."

"Hi Mom, it's Faith."

"Well, good morning, dear! It's good to hear your voice."

"Yours too, Mom. I was hoping you would answer. Are you able to have a private conversation?"

"Yes. Rachel is working at the library today. Is everything alright?" Faith hated how often her mother and daughter had to ask her that question over the years.

"Yes, Mom. Things are better than they've been in years. Did Rachel tell you about where I am and what I've been doing?"

"Yes, she said you're only weeks away from a year there. That's wonderful, dear. I'm so proud of you."

There's that word again.

"Thanks, Mom. That's actually what I wanted to talk to you about." She sent up a quick prayer. "I'll be leaving here in a little over five weeks and I would really like to move back home to Michigan. I won't if you think it would be hard on Rachel to have me there, but I really want to start over and I want a chance to have a relationship with her — with both of you — again." She held her breath as she waited for the response.

Her mother's voice was kind. "Do you think *you're* ready to be here?"

"I do. This time has been different — this time *I'm* different. This place has been amazing, and they've helped me both with the physical pain and with all the emotional baggage built up over the years. I'm completely medication-free now, Mom, and my head is clear for the first time since the accident. I know I have a lot of making up to do with both of you and that it will take time . . . I just want to be able to be a part of Rachel's life again. I've missed so much time with her."

"I'm so happy to hear that, Faith. It's all we've ever wanted and all we've ever prayed for. We all have making up to do and we'll do it together. Do you need access to treatment to stay—?"

Faith tried not to react to the emotion in her mother's voice. She was determined not to cry. "Yes, I've started doing some research and between Summit County and Traverse City, I should have access to what I need. They also offer follow-up sessions through video conferencing here for the first year, so I think it will be fine. Now that the pain is so much better, I'll look for a job right away too. I can probably even wait tables if I need to for a little while. I plan to look online over these next weeks and try to set up job interviews over the phone."

"You sound like my Faith again." She heard her mother's voice catch. "It sounds like you've been working hard on this. Rachel and I talked about it after your phone call last week, and we were both hoping you would want to come at least for a visit after you leave there. It would be wonderful if you could stay for good if you think you're ready for it. We would like to help pay for you to stay at Evelyn's bed and breakfast or the Ferrytown

Motel for a few days while you look for something permanent. We thought it would be easier for you if you had your own place to go to if it was hard on you to be here."

Her eyes stung with relief. "That sounds perfect, Mom. I'd really like that. I'll call you next week when I know dates and times, okay? Thanks, Mom. *For everything.*"

"Of course, dear. I'm looking forward to seeing you soon . . . and really having you back."

Faith exhaled as she hung up the phone. Grace Stevens was aptly named. She never seemed to feel the need to punish Faith when she messed up. She didn't do it when Faith showed up pregnant as a college student, or when she wouldn't talk about the circumstances surrounding the pregnancy, or when she couldn't get off pain medication, or when she couldn't handle being a mother, or when she lost her way with men and got into a string of relationships that were each worse than the one before.

Her mother had always held out hope for Faith to get better and had never given up on her. It was Faith who gave up, time and time again. Now that Faith was determined not to give up as she had so many times before and felt more like herself again, she felt like she had a chance to make a new life.

Chapter 9

Rick felt like a teenager, checking his phone every two minutes. Brianna and Shelby were supposed to tell his daughter about his existence yesterday, and he had been praying like a madman that she would want to get to know him.

He still didn't even have a name to pray for. Fortunately, God knew. He had always known and had always watched out for her.

Bzzz. "Finally!"

Hello Rick, My name is Rachel. Brianna and Shelby have filled me in and it appears that I'm your daughter.

He read through the email at least a dozen times. *She wants to meet me!*

∞∞∞

He hadn't breathed a word to his family about being a father, as that was too big a bomb to just drop on the people closest to him. He was supposed to go to Kingsville the next day for New

Year's Eve and had considered making the announcement then but realized he may need to put it off if he had the chance to meet her right away. After thinking about his family and their reactions, he decided he would tell them in person and make sure it was the right time to do it. He didn't want to give one of his parents a heart attack or have anyone thinking it was some elaborate joke.

Even though he had no idea what he was going to say, he was looking forward to telling his family. He wasn't necessarily a big talker, but this was the kind of news he wanted to talk to someone about. He was glad Tim had been available when he told him. Tim was the person Rick was closest to in his men's group, and he knew him to be a man who could keep a secret. Rick wasn't even ready to share it with the rest of the group until he knew more or had a conversation with Rachel.

Chapter 10

F aith was starting to get excited about her new life. It was the first time since the accident that she really felt hope about her future. She was glad that she had taken the opportunity to dive in and work through the trauma from the accident since she'd been at Healing Rock.

The after-effects of it were far-reaching and she was finally free of much of the emotional toll it had taken. That accident changed the course of her life and she needed to do a lot of grieving over the losses it brought about.

She had been a young single mother working hard to make a good life for herself and her two-year-old daughter despite being left by the love of her life when she told him she was pregnant. Her mind had been set that she was not going to be a statistic and that her daughter was going to thrive. Up to the day of the accident, she had been succeeding in what she set out to do.

She had taken a job at the university after graduation so that she could have access to close housing and childcare. Her job in the Admissions office doing marketing and administrative work was going well, and she truly enjoyed it. She was on her way back from giving a presentation on a snowy March Tuesday when a car in front of her spun out and started a nine-car pileup that changed her life.

From that point on, life headed downhill. The constant back

and leg pain, the brain fog from the painkillers, and the nagging anxiety and depression completely changed her outlook on life.

She gradually withdrew from her friendships, her mother, her church, and especially God. As hard as she had tried not to withdraw from Rachel, it was impossible not to as all of her energy went into just getting through each day. She knew Rachel was not getting the stability that she needed, so when her mother asked to take her when she was ten, Faith agreed. It was the only way she could see to give Rachel anything close to what she'd had when she was growing up.

Eventually without her daughter there to motivate her or be a reminder of why she worked so hard, she gave up on trying to be the person she once was. She was so angry at God for allowing her to get pregnant, get dumped, and get into the accident that she had rejected Him and everything she had known and followed about His ways. Her self-image was so damaged by that point that she stopped looking for a love like she had experienced with Rachel's father and settled for men who took her for granted and cheated on her.

She could look back on those days now with less tears, not because she was zoned out on painkillers as in the past, but because she had worked through much of the grief and the guilt. Psychotherapy groups, prayer time, and even music and movement therapy had worked together to give her a sense of strength and peace that she had been missing for years. Between that and the treatments addressing the chronic pain, she felt ready to try again.

She was ready to *live* again.

Chapter 11

Rick loved the freedom he felt when he flew his own plane. The tiny Cessna was his pride and joy, and he loved being able to pick up and go any time weather permitted. It also made the trip to Grand Rapids much quicker, especially on holidays.

He didn't fly as much in the winter months because the weather could change his plans so easily, but he loved the challenge involved. He had to stay as alert as he had on missions in the Air Force, but instead of enemy fire, he had to watch for wind shifts and ice pellets. At least weather wasn't trying to kill him.

Climbing into the little Cessna after flying the 747's he flew for work felt like hopping into a sports car after driving a tour bus. The landscape below was covered in a fresh blanket of snow, as was typical of this time of year. Everything from downtown Grand Rapids to the small farming communities near the airport looked so peaceful. It was like the world was at rest.

The tiny airport in Kingsville was well-kept and the runways were always cleared as he approached. He had to will himself to stay on his flight plan when what he wanted to do was continue north to Hideaway. That trip was going to have to wait for a week because Rachel had asked for time to absorb the news and feel ready.

You can wait seven days. She's been waiting twenty-five years.

His father would be picking him up and he was glad to have the time with him. He hadn't decided if he was going to tell any of the family about Rachel just yet, but he wasn't sure he could hold it in, either. He was going to be meeting his daughter for the first time in a week and could hardly contain himself. Spending the next two days with the family without telling them might be asking a little too much of himself.

He had already mapped out both the flight plan and driving route to get from Chicago to Hideaway. The weather was supposed to be clear, which wouldn't help the ski lodges much but suited his purposes just fine. Being Michigan, he couldn't depend on weather forecasts, and he was prepared to make alternative plans if needed. He made some calls and got good reports about the tiny airport in Hideaway, so he decided to risk flying in there.

The irony that his first trip to Hideaway was to see his daughter now instead of her mother twenty-six years ago was not lost on him.

It occurred to him that he hadn't discussed Faith with Rachel or her friends. He didn't know if she lived in Hideaway or if she would even come along with Rachel when they met.

His chest tightened when he thought about her. The torrent of anger he wanted to unleash on her for keeping his daughter from him almost scared him. He was used to keeping his emotions in check and being prepared for dealing with any situation that arose on an airplane, but thinking about her and what she had done made his blood boil.

He had apologized for his part in their slip-up more than once, and he had thought she accepted the apology and knew how badly he felt. He couldn't imagine that she would hold it against him to the point that she would deny him his daughter. It seemed so out of character for the sweet and feisty girl he had been so in love with.

What did you know? You were just a dumb twenty-two-year-old kid.

He was glad it was time to land the plane so he could put Faith out of his mind. He'd had plenty of practice doing just that over the years.

It should have gotten easier by now.

∞∞∞

When he walked into his sister's house, the crowd was fully engaged in the football game but took their eyes off the screen long enough to deliver holiday hugs to him. The kids even put their phones down to greet him, so he was feeling extra confident in his declaration to Brianna and Shelby that they would vouch for him.

"What's that look in your eye?" Debbie, Rick's younger sister, was always way too perceptive.

"It's New Year's Eve and I'm here with my family. There's a football game on the TV and a pot of chili on the stove. If that's not enough to put a twinkle in the eye of a simple guy like me, I don't know what is." He gave her a squeeze and a kiss on the cheek.

Note to self: don't let her get you alone if you're going to keep it to yourself. She'll pull it out of you like she always does.

"Yeah, right. What's her name?"

Rachel. Her name is Rachel.

He purposely sat on the couch between the kids so she couldn't follow him.

He loved football. No matter who was on the field, if there was a game on, he would watch it. Today, it might as well have been a paint drying documentary. He couldn't focus on much else but his upcoming meeting. He cheered when everyone else did and let the game prevent more grilling from his sister.

When the game was over, he busied himself with the kids and they showed him their presents. Sixteen-year-old Bryce had gotten a virtual reality headset, so they took turns skydiving into the Grand Canyon and floating through outer space. Eighteen-year-old Candace had gotten some new graphic design software and entertained herself designing logos to put on the dating profile she was trying to get Rick to create.

"Come on, Uncle Rick. You need a woman. A new relationship would be good for you."

If only she knew about my new relationship.

He pictured Candace the first time he saw her. She was so tiny and fragile that he was terrified he would break her. He had just sat like a stone statue and stared at the two-day-old infant in amazement. Now she was a college freshman with a strong will and sweet spirit. She had a close relationship with her father. What would she be like if she had grown up thinking her father had abandoned her?

He excused himself for a quick, brisk walk around the block, claiming a leg cramp. He needed to stop avoiding the possibility that Rachel only wanted to meet with him face to face so that she could tell him off and slap him. It was entirely possible that his first chance to meet her would be his last.

"God, I can't do this alone. She's gone her whole life not knowing me. If Faith didn't even want me to know about her, she must have passed on a pretty terrible story about me. As far as Rachel knows, I'm a real jerk."

His mind went to scary places when he thought about what had changed in Faith to go from telling him she loved him and would wait for him when he left for deployment to keeping a daughter from him. He hadn't even realized how dark it had gotten outside until he saw the headlights from behind.

Debbie pulled up beside him. "Come on, Ricky. Get in the car. You've been walking around out here for an hour."

Instead of turning around to return to her house after he got in, she pulled over to the side of the road. She put the car in park, unfastened her seat belt, and turned toward him, waiting.

"Are you going to tell me what's going on? First you looked like you had some kind of exciting secret and now you've been walking around for an hour in the dark when it's thirty-three degrees out and starting to snow. Spill it."

He sighed deeply and looked her in the eye. "I have a daughter."

"*What*!? What do you mean, you have a daughter?"

He pulled out his phone and handed it to her. "This is what came to me at twelve-thirty a.m. Christmas morning while I was lying in a hotel room in Berlin."

"Oh my gosh, Ricky. Have you talked to her?"

"No, when I finally heard from her directly, she said she didn't want to have a conversation over email and asked me to go up to Hideaway to meet with her." He told her about the emails and conversation with her friends that got him to the point of getting to hear from her.

"I keep going back and forth from being excited to start a relationship with her to terrified that she won't want one with me. You witnessed both of those things today."

"Who is the mother of this daughter?"

He choked on her name. "Faith. The one I dated during senior year at Central, before I left for Iraq."

Debbie was shocked and incensed. "She never told you? What kind of woman would do that?"

He rubbed his eyes and ran his hands through his hair. "I don't know. Either she wasn't the woman I thought she was or something happened that made her decide I was a terrible guy who shouldn't be able to raise his child."

"Wait, wasn't she the Christian one you were so crazy about? I remember talking about her at the time — you said she was saving herself for marriage. How did this even *happen*?"

"It wasn't supposed to happen. We were being careful with not letting things get too far. It was the night before I was leaving to go to Iraq and she was distraught and I was terrified and it just happened. We were young and in love and afraid and we didn't care about anything else that night."

"Wow."

"We both regretted it, she because it was a commitment she'd made to God and me because it was important to her, and we talked about it and swore it wouldn't happen again. I sent her a letter as soon as I was able to, asking her to marry me as soon as humanly possible. She never answered it."

He squeezed his eyes shut to stop the memory. "And twenty-six years later I've gotten an email that I'm a father and I'm meeting with a daughter who may or may not want to get to know me in a few days."

Debbie reached across the console to hug her brother. Then she prayed for him, for her new niece, and for Faith.

"Let's keep this between us for now, okay, sis? I don't want to get anyone's hopes up until I know if any of us will have a chance to get to know her."

"Of course. Now I understand why the topic of Faith was always off limits with you. Just remember, you don't know what's going to happen. You messed up, but look what God brought out of it. A person. A *daughter*." She grinned through her tears. "He's done a big work in your life over the past few years and He's got this. Let's go celebrate a new year. This might be the best one of your life."

Chapter 12

F aith wasn't sure why she was bothering looking for jobs so early in January when everyone was just coming back from vacation. There wasn't much to see, but she had set up a schedule for herself and was committed to following it. One of the things on the daily schedule was searching for jobs, so she was searching.

She was open to pretty much anything, which should have made her search easier, but so far, hadn't. Thankfully she had enough physical relief that if she had to go back to waiting tables for a short time to get some immediate cash, she could.

So far it had been easier finding medical professionals in the area than jobs. There were a few chiropractors that looked promising, along with a couple of naturopaths.

She wasn't going back to pill pushers if she could help it. *They're the ones who got me into this mess. Well, the physical mess, at least. I let them because I didn't know there were other options.*

She was sticking to her daily schedule pretty well and was even doing the journaling she'd committed to. It had helped over the months she had been there as she worked to unravel the patterns she had developed in her relationships with her daughter, with her mother, with men, and with God. In her shame and despair, she had gradually shut down and distanced herself from all that was good over the years.

That was all changing now.

When she first started coming out of the fog, she knew the relationship she had to start with was with God. Her descent into what she had become had started with her anger toward Him and her rejection of everything she had once believed. She blamed Him for her pregnancy, the accident, and eventually all the choices she made in the wake of her life falling apart.

Even when she came to Healing Rock, she wasn't drawn *by* the Christian aspect of the program — she was drawn there *despite* it. She wasn't even drawn by the addiction treatment. She refused to call herself addicted because she *needed* the pain killers to get through the day. It was the program they offered that dealt with chronic physical problems using multiple approaches that got her through the door. Once there, the rest followed.

They never required attendance at the Bible studies or prayer groups and she didn't start going until she was into her third month. She sat in what looked like the farthest corner, as shame-filled, angry, and afraid people do, and just listened.

When the chaplain spoke about anger and fear and guilt, she felt as if he was reading her mind. One thing she didn't hear him say was that it was all her fault or that she would have to somehow make everything up to God.

She also didn't hear that she had to do it all *alone*.

Chaplain Dave spoke about God's grace and healing. He talked about Peter a *lot* and Faith related to every word. She had never denied Christ by her words, but she had by her lifestyle. When she finally came to see that He was inviting her back just as He had invited Peter back, she started feeling hope. When, a few months later, she came to see that Jesus had later used Peter in powerful ways to spread His message of hope and redemption, she started feeling a sense of mission and purpose.

She was going to take her life back and she was going to help others do the same.

∞∞∞

Her first order of business and priority now was to rebuild her relationship with Rachel. It was hard to accept that there was nothing she could do to undo the damage she'd done to her.

She had finally accepted that she had made the best decision she could for Rachel when she gave custody of her to her mother, instead of beating herself up as she'd always done. She finally realized that by beating herself up for being imperfect and having struggles, she convinced herself that she couldn't do better. Over time she stopped *trying* to do better.

Her relationship with Rachel needed to start over, as adults. She read and re-read *Boundaries* until the book was falling apart and she practically had it memorized.

Once she got through her to-do list for the day, she pulled out her folder with her dream project in it. It was her reward for doing all the things she had to do. She got lost in it and spent the next two hours making plans.

Chapter 13

It felt like there were two fighter jets in a dog fight in Rick's stomach as he took off from Midway and headed north to meet Rachel. He had always loved flying along the Lake Michigan shoreline and the terrain helped soothe his nerves.

The white beaches dotted with tiny towns and bluffs, along with the occasional dune, were spectacular. God was in an especially good mood when He made Lake Michigan. Rick had flown this route a hundred times on his way to Mackinac Island or Charlevoix, but everything looked different now. The white snow contrasted with the trees and the deep blue of the lake and looked picture perfect.

Faith had told him all about Hideaway and Summit County, but he had never visited. After she broke up with him, he put it on his list of places to avoid because he didn't want to run the risk of running into her.

"Lord, please don't make me have to see her on this trip. Please let this trip be the first of many and please let it be about Rachel and me getting to know each other. Please get her to give me a chance."

He touched down on the small runway and exhaled.

"Here we go."

∞∞∞

He had emailed Rachel and told her his ETA so that she could pick him up. He walked out to the parking lot and looked around. After a moment, a small SUV pulled out of a parking space and pulled around.

When both the driver's and passenger's side doors opened up, he took a sharp breath. When he saw that instead of Faith, the second person was a man, he exhaled. *She brought muscle. At least it's not Faith.*

He was struck and gulped in air as she got out of the car and he saw the familiar dark blonde hair and brown eyes. *She looks so much like her mother.*

"Rachel? I'm Rick."

He felt like an idiot extending his hand to the person he should have met in a delivery room. He wanted so badly to hug her but didn't want to scare her off. She shook his hand and his heart melted a little at her touch.

"Hi. Thank you for coming all this way to meet me. This is my fiancé, Derek." She gestured to the man at her side, who quickly extended his hand.

Direct gaze, good eye contact, strong handshake, came along with her. He may be worthy.

"We made arrangements to meet at my church so we would have privacy. I hope that's okay with you."

"It's perfect." *Maybe God will bless this meeting if it's happening in His house.*

The ride was short and he was glad that Derek made conversation. Rachel's silence was deafening. The topic of the plane was always a good source of small talk and he was glad to answer questions he'd answered a thousand times.

The road from the airport toward town wound around the runway and had vast open spaces. It reminded him of Kingsville.

When they turned onto the highway that led into town, he saw why people loved Hideaway. The gateway was at the top of the last of several large rolling hills, and as they drove through it, the town below spread out before them like a postcard. The old white church with the tall steeple was just a few short blocks down. It reminded him of many of the old churches he had grown up around, churches with history.

When they walked in, they were greeted by a man who appeared to know and love Rachel.

"Pastor Ray, this is my— Rick Weston. Rick, this is Pastor Ray."

"Welcome, Rick. Rachel, I put on the tea kettle for you downstairs. Derek, I've got coffee for us up in my office. We'll be up there if you need us."

He and Derek both gave Rachel a look as if waiting for her approval before they left. *More protective people in her life. Thank You, God.*

Rachel thanked them and started down the stairs while they headed up to the upper level. Derek gave her a reassuring touch on her shoulder as he walked away. *You're earning points with me, young man.*

He was thankful for the bottles of water in the fridge, both to give him something to hold onto and to give his parched mouth a chance to work properly.

"Thank you for letting me come to meet you, Rachel. I'm sure you have questions. I'm not sure I have the answers, but I'll tell you anything you want to know."

"I do have a lot of questions, but I think I need to start with the one I've always asked." She paused for a long moment. "Where have you been?"

A slap would have been easier to take. As much as he'd tried to prepare himself for this moment, he wasn't prepared for the pain in her eyes.

"I— I'm not sure what your mother told you about me, but I never knew about you until I got that email on Christmas. I'm so sorry." He felt tears stinging his eyes and willed them away so he could continue. "I know you don't know me and have no reason to believe what I say, but as God is my witness, I had no idea your mother was pregnant."

She looked skeptical. "Um, forgive me, but how could that be? Weren't you in a relationship with her? She wasn't the kind of girl to sleep around from what I've heard, so you must have been special. Unless—" A look of horror covered her face.

"No, Rachel. *No.* It wasn't that. I loved your mom and wanted to marry her. I never forced myself on her." The thought made him want to vomit. "You were conceived in love by two kids who lost control on the last night they saw each other."

Her brow furrowed. "Why was that the last night you saw each other?"

"Has she not told you any of this? Is she— is she *not with us* anymore?"

"She's alive, she's just never talked about you. Please, go on. I'd like to hear this directly from you."

"It happened the night before I left for the Air Force and Iraq. Our emotions got the best of us and . . ." He trailed off, trying to tell the story without getting caught up in it again.

He took a swig of water and looked her in the eye. "I loved your mother more than I've ever loved anyone, before or since. I was never happier than when I was with her and I thought we were going to get married. I *asked her* to marry me and I apologized for things getting out of hand." *And I never heard from her again.*

Rachel stared at the floor for a long moment that seemed like an eternity. "This is a lot to take in. I need some time to process before I have more questions about that. So you never married or had kids?"

"No. I had a few long relationships, but none of them set my world on fire. After what I had with your mom I didn't want to settle for less, but I also didn't want to hurt like that, so I probably only dated women who *wouldn't* set my world on fire." That realization hit him as he said it.

She was staring intently at the wall behind him. "I'm familiar with that tactic."

"It's not really my place and I know I haven't earned the right to ask, but does Derek set your world on fire?"

She smiled broadly for the first time since they'd met. It was the involuntary smile of a woman in love.

It was the smile he'd seen a thousand times on a face that looked a lot like hers a long, long time ago.

"Yes, he does."

She became quiet again and looked at the floor, as if trying to figure out what to say next.

Please just don't say goodbye.

"Rachel, I realize you have a lot to take in. I've been praying my guts out since I got that email and asking God to give me a chance with you. I don't know if you want to keep talking today, but if you don't, can we please talk again?"

She gripped the arms of her chair. "I want to talk more, but I'm trying to take everything in. You've given me a lot to think about and I need to have a big conversation with my mom. She's a bit . . . fragile . . . and I have to be careful with bringing something like this up with her."

Fragile? Faith?

His heart sank. "Is she okay?"

As angry as he was at her for keeping Rachel from him, he didn't want anything bad to happen to her. And 'fragile' was not a word that he ever would have associated with Faith.

Rachel seemed hesitant. "She's had a hard life."

He wasn't sure what to say as she stared again at the floor with a look of utter sadness.

What is going on with Faith?

His stomach growled and broke up the silence that had descended. She exhaled and said, "I'm hungry, too. Would you like to have lunch with Derek and me? I would like to keep talking."

Absolutely!

"Absolutely I would."

∞∞∞

They left Hideaway and drove several miles to what must have been the next town over on the other end of a large inland lake. *She probably doesn't want to run into her mother with me. That makes two of us.*

He tried to keep the conversation light and enjoy the ride. It was easy to talk about the beauty of the area as they drove back over the rolling hills and occasionally saw glimpses of the inland lake with the deep blue water. He imagined it in the summer, full of water skiers and sailboats, and hoped he would get a chance to see it.

Derek once again made most of the conversation in the car as Rachel appeared to be deep in thought. "I almost left this place once. It would have been the biggest mistake of my life." He reached across the seat and took Rachel's hand.

It was good to see the connection they had. If she decided not to see him after today, he had the feeling she was in good hands.

"What made you almost leave?"

"I lost the girl of my dreams." He grinned as he held up her hand, showing the engagement ring. "It's okay. I got her back."

The look on her face could only be described as adoration as she looked at him.

Rick couldn't imagine what would cause the two of them to break up, but it was none of his business so he didn't ask. "From what I can tell, Derek, you've got a great one there." *I sure hope you honor her better than I honored her mother.*

Downtown Lakes End had a different kind of charm to it than

Hideaway. It was even smaller and, from what he could see of it, only had two blocks with businesses on them.

He had been in Chicago long enough that he had almost forgotten that towns could be separated by hills and even miles rather than simply cross streets and stoplights. He could barely see the other end of the lake, and there was only a small amount of ice formed at the end closest to town.

They went into a small, dark restaurant where Derek requested a booth in the back. Rachel looked as if she was struggling with what she wanted to say.

Rick decided to break the ice. "I'll bet you didn't think you would have such a fast match on GenealogyWeb when you did the DNA test a few weeks ago, Rachel. I had forgotten that I had even submitted a DNA swab. My niece convinced me to join when she was working on a school project a couple of years ago."

"Your niece — that's right. I'd like to hear about your family. I didn't think I would find *you* or any family members through the site. I was just hoping for some genetic information. I wanted to know about your side of the family because I didn't know anything."

Ouch. She wasn't looking for me, only information.

"Well, I hope you weren't too disappointed to get me in the deal, too. I'm sure it was quite a shock." He tried to keep his voice light and hide the disappointment and fear in it.

Her hand flew to her mouth. "I'm sorry, I didn't mean it like that. I think I'm still in shock about finding you. I hoped to find out *about* you but never expected to find the actual living, breathing person."

"It's ok. This is weird for both of us."

Imagine my shock. You knew you had a father.

She sounded sincere when she spoke again. "I'd like to hear about your family. I'm still absorbing the fact that I have relatives I don't know. Have you told them about . . . this?"

"I've only told my sister about you so far. I was going to tell everyone when I was with them over New Year's, but I didn't want to get their hopes up if you only wanted to meet in person so you could slap me in the face and tell me to get lost."

Derek almost choked on his drink. "Trust me, you do not want her mad at you. She has no qualms about telling people to get lost." She playfully jabbed him in the ribs with her elbow even as she gave him that same adoring look he'd seen earlier.

"I've spent the last twenty-five years lost, so I hope I'll get a chance to stay around." He ventured a shy smile toward Rachel and when she returned it, his heart soared.

∞∞∞

The flight home was much different than the one there. He felt like he had enough lift and thrust in his spirit that he didn't even need the plane.

Rachel had agreed to meet again soon and to be in touch through email. She seemed to genuinely want to meet his family, even though they both agreed it was too soon. They would talk about a specific time the next time they met.

Every time he thought about 'next time,' his heart skipped a beat. He didn't know if he had won Rachel over yet, but she seemed to be giving him a chance. *That's all I ask for.*

He made a quick overnight stop in Kingsville to make the an-

NEW BEGINNINGS IN SUMMIT COUNTY

nouncement to his family on his way back to Chicago. He still had a couple of days before he had to report for his next four-day trip for work and decided a night with family was just what he needed.

Everyone was, of course, shocked. Candace had gotten the notification of a potential cousin but had been so busy that she hadn't read the email. His parents were ready to go right back to the plane to go to meet Rachel but understood the wisdom in letting the family introductions unfold slowly.

Chapter 14

Faith had a long but productive day. She started with her first aftercare planning conference with the physical therapist and massage therapist to put together her plan for the exercises she could do at home and at a fitness center to maintain the flexibility and strength she had gained throughout the months at Healing Rock. They were both as pleased as Faith was with her progress, though less shocked.

Even though Faith came to the program because of their success rate with chronic pain, she didn't expect to be able to walk and move without the horrible degree of pain that had plagued her for years. When they first told her that the opiates were contributing to the back pain in addition to relieving it, she thought they were crazy. When they started working on inflammation and using chiropractic, acupuncture, and massage treatments and she started feeling some relief, she started believing that they may be onto something. As she was weaned off the meds and started eating an anti-inflammatory diet and taking supplements, she found that what they were teaching her was truth.

By the time of the planning meeting, she was not only a believer in the possibilities for people suffering from chronic pain but an advocate of their methods. She looked forward to the day when she could spread the kind of hope and relief she had gained.

After the meeting, it was time to put in her hours in the office.

One of the many perks at Healing Rock was the ability to do work there that could be put on a resume. Since taking ownership was a pillar of the program, everyone there had a job, and upon completion of the program, the job could be put on a resume.

They tried to match participants with jobs they already had skills or an aptitude for whenever possible, and since she had a degree with a double major in Marketing and Communications and had been successful in a career before life spiraled out of control, she was able to work in the front office. She'd even done a bit of networking and public speaking about the program. Everyone she spoke to assumed she was simply an employee, not a client.

When she finally got around to creating a LinkedIn profile, the "job" would make her look marketable indeed. She added that to her to-do list for later.

She had learned enough about the business end of the program that she felt confident that one day she could duplicate it and help others like herself. She wasn't sure how long it would be before she could attempt such a feat, but she kept the dream in her sights to have a long-term goal to aim toward. The folder she kept with ideas and plans to make it a reality was expanding daily, and her reward at the end of long days was to open that folder and work on her plans.

She had even started looking online at properties around Summit County for the treatment center she wanted to create. It would be a while before she could do anything to start it, but she had always been a planner and knew there would need to be a lot of groundwork done beforehand. The fundraising, marketing, and business planning ideas she was working on were forming the foundation for the entire project.

Time was ticking down to her new life and she couldn't wait.

She only had four weeks to go until life would fully begin again.

Chapter 15

Rick spent his downtime in Budapest working on the class that had just started. He was glad to have a distraction even though it took willpower to focus.

He had started taking classes several years before and found it helpful for passing the mandatory rest hours, both at home and when he was in other parts of the world. Flying to international destinations was prestigious and made him a good living, but there was a lot of time in hotel rooms and strange cities and he had seen other pilots make choices with how they spent that time that destroyed their families and sometimes their careers. He had also seen others use the time wisely, and those were the footsteps he wanted to follow in.

It had taken a bit of time to adjust to a classroom consisting of a laptop and room service in a nice hotel, but he eventually got into the rhythm of it and found it enjoyable. When he quit drinking, he found that he had too much free time while traveling and upped the course load.

He was almost done with his second master's degree, this time in Business Administration. It would come in handy whenever he decided to take the plunge and start a charter service or some other business after he tired of the climb, cruise, descend, land life. He knew he would never tire of *flying*, but his Cessna or a mid-sized charter plane would satisfy the urge to soar above the clouds.

It was hard concentrating on the coursework in front of him. He had run into Trina in the pilots' lounge before leaving for Budapest and kept repeating the conversation in his mind. She was glowing brighter than the huge new engagement ring she was sporting on her left hand. Noticing that Rick had a glow too, she asked him if he was also in a new relationship.

"No, just some exciting new things going on in my life. Someday I'll fill you in, but it's too soon now. I'm glad for you, though. I've never seen you look this happy."

"I've never felt loved like this."

He winced, even as he knew it was true.

He looked at her sheepishly. "I'm sorry about that. I've realized recently that my heart hasn't really been available to give to anyone for a very long time."

"There's no need for apologies, Rick. I always thought someone else had your heart even though you denied it, and it was okay with me because I wasn't ready to risk giving you mine either. I hope yours is freed up now and that you can find that special someone. Believe me, it's worth it."

Before he could respond, she was paged. It was a nice thought, but there was only one relationship on his horizon for now.

He forced his attention back to the computer screen. He really just wanted the trip over so that he could get back to Hideaway for another visit with Rachel. This time she had invited him to the home she shared with her grandmother.

As much as he was looking forward to meeting Grace Stevens, he was certain she wouldn't have a high opinion of him. He hoped he could win her over so that she wouldn't think he was some cad who got her daughter pregnant and then left her in the lurch.

In the two weeks since their last visit, Rachel had kept to her word to stay in touch through email and they had written back and forth fairly regularly. She hadn't said anything more about Faith or his relationship with her, and he had followed her lead. They had talked about her meeting his family after his next visit to Hideaway, and he got the impression Rachel was looking forward to it too.

Chapter 16

F aith wasn't sure what to make of it when she got a message that Rachel wanted her to call, and she did so at the first opportunity. When Rachel said she wanted to come for a visit, Faith was thrilled, but nervous. It was a long way to come to spend a few hours visiting.

She didn't know if Rachel wanted to see her to see if she was really better or if she wanted to talk to her in person to ask her not to return to Hideaway. Rachel had sounded nervous on the phone and acted as if something was on her mind. Faith prayed while she waited and asked God to guide the conversation and to keep the relationship moving forward.

Rachel was a sight for sore eyes. It had been well over a year since they'd been together, and they hugged each other as if it had been twenty years. In a way, it felt like it had been. It had been twenty-three years since she'd been with her daughter without being on some type of medication that messed with her head.

"You look beautiful, Sweetheart. You look happy and healthy."

"So do you, Mom. I wanted to see for myself that you were doing as well as you sounded on the phone. I also thought it would be a good idea if we talked about some things before you move back home."

Okay, she's not saying she doesn't want me to move back home. Thank You, Lord.

"Of course. That sounds good."

"I know we need to start fresh and I'm looking forward to doing that. If we're going to start fresh, though, I think we need to talk about some things we've never talked about."

Faith was ready. She was prepared to apologize for letting her life go so far off the rails and for taking Rachel with her. She was prepared to apologize for not being there for her and for creating so much instability for her.

"There are a few things, but what I really want to know about right now is my father."

Faith's heart sank. *Rick.*

She was not prepared for that topic. *Well, you'd better get prepared.*

She had always dreaded and avoided this day. Not wanting to tell her daughter that her father didn't want her, she had said nothing about him.

She took a gulp of water. "Okay, where do you want me to start?"

"How about at the beginning? You never told me his name or anything about your relationship and I want to hear your story."

"Okay. You're right. It's past time and I'm sorry I've never told you about this. I didn't know what to say, so I said nothing."

She took as deep a breath as her suddenly constricted lungs allowed. "We met at the end of fall semester during my junior year at Central. I was waitressing at the Pizza Shack and he and another guy came in for pizza. The other guy had this ROTC swagger and really thought he was something — I think he had watched *Top Gun* a few too many times. He kept asking me out and I kept saying no and wishing his friend would. When they left, the friend — your father — snuck a note with an apology for his friend's boorish behavior on a napkin stuffed with a huge tip onto the table.

"He started coming in regularly and we became friends. When *he* finally asked me out, like a *gentleman*, I said yes. We spent all of our time together and were really in love. That was the best eight months of my life. He treated me like a princess and remained a gentleman. He respected my commitment not to have sex before marriage and he said he would wait for me. We weren't officially engaged, but we talked about marriage as if it was a given."

Faith took a drink of water to settle her nerves and wash away the tears. It had been years since she had allowed herself to think about those days.

"He had graduated and was already enlisted in the Air Force. When he received his orders, we were both scared to death. The Gulf War had just happened and he was going to be sent on peacekeeping missions, which sounded to me like combat by another name. We told ourselves that he would only be there for a few months, but we knew what could happen in those months. It was awful."

She cleared her throat and tried to figure out a delicate way to continue. "Do you really want to hear this, Rachel?"

Rachel nodded. "It's okay. I'm an adult and I've known you had me out of wedlock since I was a child. I knew you lived with some of your boyfriends after I moved in with Grandma. Please, go on. I think it's important that I hear this."

"It was different with him — he wasn't like any of the men you knew. Everything was pure in our relationship. Everything was so good."

She wiped a tear from her eye as memories of feeling so loved crept in.

"The night before he left, we had just gotten news that a guy he had met was killed on one of the types of missions he was about to be sent to go on. We were both shaken up and afraid. We cried together and we . . . didn't stop that night. We both felt bad about it after."

She realized what that may have sounded like and looked her daughter in the eye. "I don't regret it, even though it was wrong. It's how you came to be and you've been the best thing to ever happen in my life. You're the ultimate proof to me that God works everything for good."

Rachel just nodded.

"Anyway, I got a letter from him apologizing again for it, telling me he loved me, and asking me to marry him as soon as possible. Letters took a while back then and his letter arrived the day after I found out I was pregnant. I wrote back, telling him I loved him and wanted to marry him too, and I never heard from him again. After checking and rechecking the mailbox for months, I accepted that he didn't want me anymore and that he had moved on."

She purposely left out the part about telling him she was pregnant. Rachel had had enough pain in her life without knowing that her father had rejected her.

She asked God for forgiveness for the omission and continued. "So that's pretty much it. I had you and was doing pretty well as a single mom until the accident happened and changed everything. After the accident and the pain and the drugs, I rejected God the way I had been rejected and life took a horrible turn."

Rachel was quiet and looked at the floor. She had always been a contemplative child and when she got quiet, Faith could almost hear the engines in her brain turning. As she grew older, and more damaged, the contemplation sometimes turned into shutting down. Faith hoped today it was contemplation.

"Mom ... I met Rick and he said he didn't know about me. Why didn't you tell him?"

He said what!? How could he?

Faith felt like the bottom just dropped out of the room.

"You met Rick?"

"We're both members of a genealogy site and were contacted about a parent-child DNA match. He flew up to meet me last week and he said he didn't know about me — he seemed sincere."

When she looked up, Faith saw something she had never seen enough of in Rachel's eyes: hope.

Sincere, huh? She asked God for strength to once again lie for him to protect her daughter.

"I'm sorry, Sweetheart."

Rachel hugged her and held her tight.

"It's okay, Mom. I'm sorry you had to do all that alone. I know you did your best. You always did your best."

"Do you know that I was doing my best when I agreed to let Grandma raise you? I was trying to protect you from what I was becoming." She stroked Rachel's long hair like she had when she was a child. "I couldn't be the kind of mom I wanted to be or give you what you needed and I just gave up. I'm so sorry. I didn't know how to get out of the hole I had dug myself into and the only thing I could think to do to save you was hand you up to Grandma. Do you understand?"

"I do. You did the best thing you could think to do. I love you and I've forgiven you, Mom. I hope you'll forgive me too for not always reaching back to you."

"Oh, Sweetheart."

The two Stevens ladies, who both hated emotions and hated crying, cried on each other's shoulders. Faith pulled back and gave a little laugh as she wiped a tear from Rachel's cheek.

"We're crying. We *hate* crying."

Rachel laughed too. "I know. I think we needed this, though."

She picked up the box of tissues and set it between them. "Thank you for telling me your story, Mom. Do you mind if I change the subject to something happy?"

"Please do."

"Derek and I are getting married in five weeks and we want you to be there."

Chapter 17

Rick was feeling good about how the important conversations had been going, but he still had one very important one to prepare for.

This time, he did use paper and this time he did crumple it up and throw it at the wall. After doing that several times, he went to the gym and lifted weights.

It didn't help.

He needed to talk to Faith. She was the only one who could provide the answers he needed.

He didn't dare ask Rachel for her number. Those two relationships needed to be kept separate and he sensed something in Rachel when Faith's name came up. She seemed sad and protective when it came to Faith, and he got the feeling that when she said Faith was fragile and had a hard life, it was an understatement. He could feel compassion for her chipping away at his anger.

The next morning at men's group, he shared the whole tale and asked them to be praying for both his relationship with Rachel and his future conversation with Faith. He had no idea what to expect with her and wondered just what had gone on in her life since he last knew her.

Their last conversation was the morning he left for Iraq. They had talked about feeling bad about what had happened the night before and committing to not letting it happen again. He thought they were on the same page when he left.

When he wrote to her declaring his love, proposing, and asking her to marry him when he was on leave, he had also apologized again for not stopping when he knew she might regret it. He took full responsibility and vowed that he would never let things get out of control again.

He wondered if she didn't believe him. He wondered if she felt so tarnished by that night, by *him*, that she went down a bad path in life afterward. A wave of guilt washed over him.

She was the one who was committed to no sex before marriage, but he was the one who was supposed to be her protector. He had held to his promise not to push things and everything was mutual that night, but he should have had the strength when she didn't. *Lord, please tell me I didn't ruin her life.*

For the first time in over two years, he wanted a drink. He grabbed his keys and phone. He would call his sponsor on the way to the gym.

∞∞∞

"It feels good to cream you in racquetball again."

"It feels good to let you. Whose face were you picturing on that ball?"

"Would you think ill of me if I said it was a woman?"

"Better the racquetball than her real face. What did she do?"

"Kept my daughter from me for twenty-five years."

"Oh, man. I'm sorry. Want me to let you beat me again?"

Rick chuckled. "No, I'm good now. Thanks for meeting me here. It's been a long time since I've wanted a drink. The urge wasn't that bad, but the fact that it was there at all sent me into a nosedive."

"I get it — I've been there. Do you want to go find a meeting?"

"I just had one."

Chapter 18

Faith was still reeling from the visit with Rachel two days later. It took a lot out of her to tell her story, remember feelings she had long since buried, and to cover up for Rick *again*.

She was surprised by the intensity of the anger she felt — she had forgiven him for leaving her and dismissing Rachel, but hearing that he was lying about it infuriated her. Rachel had such hope in her eyes when she talked about him, and Faith wasn't going to steal it from her.

She *was*, however, going to find him and have a word with him.

Now that she was set to move back to Hideaway in a few weeks and there was a chance that Rachel would invite him to her wedding and that he would be making regular visits, it was inevitable that she would see him. She was going to be pro-active and give him a piece of her mind.

I really am back to myself.

∞∞∞

Faith tried but failed to remain calm as she talked to Brandy about Rick. Her hurt was still raw and Brandy let her unload.

"How dare he act like the victim? He thinks he can *reject* her – both of us – and waltz back into her life twenty-five years later and claim ignorance? He gets to be the victim while I'm the mother who failed her?"

"Faith, take this." She handed her a note pad and pen. "I'm giving you the instructions you gave me a few weeks ago. Write down everything you want to say to him. When you finish, tear it up or bring it to me."

Faith started writing . . . and writing . . . and writing. Brandy quietly set the tissue box next to her and left the room.

Faith let out all of the anger and hurt that she had been carrying alone for twenty-six years. She wrote every word that came to mind, even the ugly ones. She tore up the papers as she went and felt freedom and release with each one.

The first letters were like an atomic bomb, telling him what a liar and a jerk he was. The next ones told him how worthless and rejected he had made her feel. Those were followed by telling him how he ruined her for other good men because he made her doubt that they existed and made her feel like less of a person.

The hardest ones were the ones where she told him what it was like for Rachel to grow up without a father. She told him how hard she worked to prevent Rachel from knowing that he didn't want her and how much she resented him coming around twenty-five years later.

She wrote until her hand felt like it was on fire and then wrote more.

She knew that she was going to need to get around to forgiveness, but she wasn't ready for that yet. Even though the intensity of her emotions was much lower after all the writing, she was still angry.

When she walked into Bible study that afternoon, Chaplain Dave said they were going to talk about forgiveness. She looked up toward heaven. *What a coincidence.*

He spoke of God's forgiveness toward His people and of the things that get in the way of people forgiving others as well as accepting His forgiveness. *I know he's right, Lord. Forgiveness is not understanding and it's not saying something wasn't bad or didn't hurt — it's cancelling a debt that can't be paid.*

Faith wanted to forgive. She knew she needed to give thought to what the chaplain said and that she needed God's help. There was no way she could do *that* on her own.

Chapter 19

Rick was hesitant and full of mixed emotions as he tapped Faith's name into the search bar. There were a few results, mostly on social media, with profile pictures of flowers or pets. *Apparently there are a lot of women named Faith Stevens out there who don't want to be found.*

Since he didn't have any social media accounts, he couldn't view anything anyway. It was just as well. He didn't want to get sidetracked before his next visit with Rachel.

He was still a bit shaken by the fact that he had even thought about drinking the other night — he thought he was past that. He'd always been an overachiever who set his mind on a goal and hit it. When he decided he was done with drinking for good, he figured that that was it.

He reminded himself that the other night wasn't like those early days of sobriety. It was a struggle back then. There were nights when he went to two meetings in a row and often when he was on the other side of the world for work, he talked to his sponsor or other friends through video conferencing each night. The other night was a temptation, but not a *struggle*.

The one thing that he treasured about his sobriety journey thus far was the path it put him on to reach God. When he finally admitted he needed to address his drinking, he had gone to a meeting at a church near his condo. He didn't understand it at the time, but it felt like home when he walked in.

He was raised in the church and in what was for all intents and purposes a Christian town, but had never made God a priority in his heart or life. Even when he and Faith started dating, he could talk the talk, but wasn't walking the walk. He thought it was good enough that he was a good guy and was moral compared to his friends.

It was Faith who loved Jesus and wanted to please Him with her life. It was she who showed him what a person who lived for God really looked like. It was also Faith whose face he put on God, though, and when she left him, that was the end of that budding relationship too.

He had shut God out completely until he came to the point of admitting that his drinking was becoming a problem and that he needed help. Fortunately, he found that just as he had been taught from a young age, God was there when people reached out to Him. Eventually he started going to the church for services, not just meetings.

He met a lot of real people with real struggles who depended on God to get them through. For the first time in his life, he understood that desire and need. For the first time in his life, God was real.

Chapter 20

Faith had been at the computer for thirty minutes. It was no surprise that Rick's number and address were unlisted, but she was shocked that he could somehow have no internet footprint whatsoever. Fortunately, she had learned a few tricks over the years and wasn't done looking.

"Bingo!"

There it was: a phone number. There was no way of knowing if it was current, but she dialed it before she lost her nerve. It went right to voice mail and when she heard his deep voice on the outgoing message, a part of her involuntarily swooned even as she felt her anger rise up. *Ugh, he's still got that voice.*

She quickly hung up the phone and was glad he hadn't answered.

Next time she needed to be more prepared. She needed to be ready to have a calm conversation and be able to be in control of her emotions and her words. She also needed to be strong and not be influenced by the effect his voice still had on her. As hard as she tried not to picture his face, she couldn't help it.

The first time he walked into the restaurant she had noticed him immediately. Even though he had that military posture and carried himself with confidence, he didn't come across as cocky. He had a big grin, and when he smiled his eyes sparkled and sent her insides melting.

She could only imagine what he must look like now. She shook her head to get rid of the thought.

I hope he's round and bald and covered with warts.

Chapter 21

Rick took in his surroundings as he sat in Rachel and Grace's living room. The rich brown walls and over-stuffed furniture made him feel like he could sit there for hours. It was much different than the cold hotel rooms he spent so much time in and even his own functionally furnished and sparsely decorated condo.

He had a hard time taking his eyes off the portrait of Rachel hanging prominently between the two windows. Rachel blushed as she told him that Derek had painted it. Rick was impressed with his skill as an artist, especially of his ability to capture Rachel's sweet essence in it. It was as if it was more than a picture — it was a *tribute*.

Grace Stevens was everything he had always heard she was, and he could see why Faith always spoke so fondly of her. She was cordial and welcoming, and it was obvious that she had a very special relationship with Rachel.

He wondered how long Rachel had lived with her and if Faith lived there too. The way Rachel spoke gave him the impression that it was just she and her grandmother there. There was no sign of Faith in the home other than a few pictures of her with Rachel when Rachel was a little girl. He had the feeling that he was missing some vital information about Faith but was determined not to bring her up if Rachel didn't.

Grace brought out some photo albums of Rachel as a preteen and teenager, which only added to the mystery. There were plenty of pictures of Rachel and Grace, but the only ones of Faith were taken on holidays.

She didn't look like the Faith he remembered. Gone was the light and laughter in her eyes and the bright smile — she looked like a ghost of her former self.

He was beginning to suspect that when Rachel said that Faith had had a hard life, it was much more than an understatement. It made his gut clench to think of her suffering, even after what she'd done to him.

Derek joined them on his lunch break from his family's insurance agency and again for dinner, and Rick was again comforted by what he observed between him and his daughter. Rick noticed that there was no talk about their upcoming wedding and he wondered if that was intentional. He knew he hadn't earned an invitation to that event, but he hoped that it was far enough away that by the time it came around, he would.

The conversation was easier on this visit and it seemed Rachel was more relaxed. He felt like they were actually getting to know each other, and that impression was confirmed when Rachel asked when she could meet his family as she dropped him off at their friend Evelyn's Bed and Breakfast, the Shoreside Inn.

"Well, that's one of the nice things about having a plane on hand — it makes the trip a pretty quick one. If you would like to fly with me, I'll take you any time you want to go."

"How about tomorrow?"

"They'll be thrilled."

∞∞∞

When they arrived at the Shoreside Inn, Rick was pleasantly surprised to meet Shelby, one of the Gatekeepers, in person. Shelby had recently returned to Hideaway after graduating from college, and she was staying with her Aunt Evelyn as she attempted to recover from a chronic illness that had made her last several years a struggle.

She and Evelyn were very hospitable, and Rick decided that this would be his regular place to stay when he visited if they would have him. The large, elegant Victorian home appeared to be undergoing some renovations and it was clear that it was a labor of love.

When Rachel left, Shelby made a point of staying in the living room and offered Rick some tea. He was glad to have a moment alone with her to tell her again how grateful he was that she and Brianna allowed him to have contact with Rachel.

She told him the DNA test and membership was actually their idea, not Rachel's. "When Brianna and I decided to get the DNA test kit and membership for Rachel, we prayed for *months* before giving it to her. We had both heard stories of families being reunited through the DNA testing and hoped that it would lead her to you. Of course, we never mentioned that to Rachel because we didn't want to get her hopes up. We figured it would take a lot longer and we were ready to do any research and digging we would need to in order to find you or your family. When we got the notification about you, we were shocked and knew it was a huge answer to prayer. Rachel needed answers."

Rick needed answers, too. *Tread lightly here, man.*

"I get the impression she didn't have any answers about me

from Faith. I also get the impression that there are a lot of things that I don't know about Faith and her life since I knew her."

Shelby looked thoughtful and seemed to choose her words carefully. "Your impression is correct about both of those things. I'm glad you're filling in the blanks for Rachel and giving her some of the answers that she's always wanted. I'm sure she'll tell you more about her mom when she's ready."

What in the world happened to Faith?

Chapter 22

Faith was enjoying the regular phone conversations she had been having with her mother. They were so close when she was growing up, and even after she had Rachel.

Grace had offered to have them live with her after Rachel was born, but Faith was determined to make it without any help. She was glad to be able to work at the university so she could establish herself and feel like she was standing on her own two feet.

When she was recovering from the accident and surgeries, Grace moved into their house for six months. She was there to take care of Rachel while Faith stayed in the hospital and rehabilitation facility and then after, when Faith was unable to lift Rachel and spent much of the time she wasn't at work either doing physical therapy or recovering from it.

Grace was concerned about the amount of pain medications the doctors were giving to Faith but deferred to their expertise. When she brought it up with Faith later, it only led to arguments. Now Faith was determined to have as clean a slate as possible with both her mother and her daughter before she moved back to their town.

"Mom, I know I've apologized a million times over the years, but I want to do it again now that I have a clear head. It's hit me like a ton of bricks over the past several months what I've put you through. A mother should never have to worry about her child's ability to just get through a day and should never have to wonder where she is living or what she is doing." She shuddered as she remembered the pain on her mother's face. "I didn't always tell you what was going on because I didn't want to worry you — or hear about how I needed to do things differently. For the first ten months I was here, I was so afraid to jinx it that I didn't tell you or Rachel where I was or that I was on the right path finally. I'm sorry — I never meant to worry you. I hope you can forgive me."

"Oh, Faith, I've already forgiven you. There's nothing we can do to change the past. I haven't done things perfectly either, and I hope you can forgive me for the times when you thought I was trying to keep Rachel from you. The best thing I could do for you was to take the best care of your daughter that I could manage."

"Of course I can, Mom. You saw more clearly than I could what she needed, and I'm grateful that you did what was best for her even when I didn't like it. I couldn't be more proud of the young woman Rachel has become, and you get all the credit for that."

She felt the tears threatening, so she changed the subject. "Speaking of Rachel, where is she today? Are she and Derek off making wedding plans?"

Grace hesitated for a moment, then said, "No, she's with Rick today — she's meeting his family."

Chapter 23

Rick had a combination of excitement and nervousness in his stomach that made it feel like the jets were back again.

It seemed unreal that he and Rachel were about to land in Kingsville to spend the day with his family. It was hard for him to believe that a month ago he didn't even know about Rachel's existence and now he was about to introduce her to her grandparents who *she* didn't know existed.

He was glad that he had decided to have her meet his parents first and spend some time with them before she met the rest of the family so that she wouldn't be overwhelmed. He felt like he was starting to get to know her and to understand her personality and could see that she went to a place inside her own mind as she processed things. Whether it was just because she was introverted or because she had been hurt deeply, he wanted to be respectful of it and wanted to make social situations easier on her. He knew he still hadn't completely won her over and suspected that she took time before extending trust to people, so he was trying to show himself worthy of that trust.

The flight down had gone well, and it was nice to be able to spend time alone with her for more than a couple of minutes. It was the first time they had had that opportunity and had been able to have conversations without others around.

He was happy to get to know her better as she told him more about her life, her work at the library, and her love of history. It was obvious that she loved what she did and loved being able to be surrounded by books, and he made a mental note to make sure to show her his mother's extensive book collection. When they landed at the Kingsville Airport, he could see the excitement on his parents' faces through the window as they tried to get their first glimpses of their new granddaughter.

They went back to their house and his mother served her famous corn chowder for lunch. She also brought out photo albums so she could show Rachel pictures of him as a child as well as pictures of the aunt, uncle, and cousin she would be meeting later in the day. Rachel seemed interested in learning about the family's history, and he hoped she wasn't feeling overwhelmed by all the attention.

He hoped he could take it as a good sign that she asked his mother questions about the family. He hoped that was an indication that she planned on letting his family be a part of her future. When his mother asked her questions about her upcoming wedding, he noticed she still carefully avoided talking about the wedding date but still had that same smile that she didn't seem to be able to help when she spoke of Derek.

He learned a little bit more about them and found out that they had broken up for three-and-a-half years and just recently reunited after realizing that what had caused the breakup was a big misunderstanding. She didn't go into specifics but alluded to the need for forgiveness and reparation.

He hoped she was better at forgiving than he was. He was also a bit envious of her for having a breakup based on a misunderstanding instead of deception. How easy it must have been to realize the misunderstanding, apologize, forgive, and walk off into the sunset together. *Well, maybe not easy, but simple.*

When his sister and her family arrived at his parents' home, he was pleasantly surprised that Candace had made a special trip home from school so that she could also meet her new cousin. He saw a lot of similarities between the two and had hoped they would get acquainted.

The visit went well and Rachel seemed to enjoy herself. After Rick's father dropped them off at the airport, Rachel turned to him.

"You have a nice family."

"*You* have a nice family."

"*Oh*." She laughed. "I guess I do." She had a nice laugh and it warmed his heart to hear it.

They talked about what a strange thing it was to have instant family members and to try to get to know their entire histories in one sitting. He encouraged her to take her time getting to know him and his family and asked her to be honest with him if he was pushing things too fast. She seemed to appreciate his acknowledgement of her need for time.

He knew she was tired when they took off to fly back to Hideaway and wasn't sure if the silence she had fallen into was from that or if she was processing.

Suddenly, she broke the silence. "I know we haven't talked about it much, but Derek and I are getting married four weeks from Saturday and we would like it if you would come to our wedding."

"I would be absolutely honored. Thank you for that, Rachel."

He managed a smile in her direction but had to focus on the instrument panel so that he wouldn't break into tears.

Thank You, God.

Chapter 24

Faith had been thinking about Rachel and Rick almost non-stop for days. She would be moving to Hideaway in a little over a week and needed to be making preparations for that, but all she could think about was the relationship that was growing between her daughter and the father who had rejected her.

She knew she couldn't prevent Rachel from getting hurt but wished she could do *something*. She didn't trust Rick as far as she could throw him and was determined to limit the damage he could do.

Her mind kept wandering to curiosity about how many other children he had and if Rachel was getting swept up into a happy family fantasy. She pictured Rick and his wife and their two-point-five children, dog, and white picket fence, and pictured them bringing Rachel into the perfect little fold.

When she realized what she was doing, she stopped herself in her tracks. Even if all that was true, it shouldn't have any bearing on her relationship with Rachel.

They had been talking every few days, and things were better than they had ever been. She and Rachel were building a completely new foundation for their relationship. That foundation would come in handy when Rachel inevitably got her heart broken by him.

This time, Faith would be there to pick up the pieces.

She called Rachel to see how the wedding plans were coming and to talk about her arrival — and to see if Rachel mentioned her new family. Rachel didn't mention the visit with her new relatives, but she sounded happy. She even sounded relaxed when she talked about her upcoming wedding.

They were keeping things very simple and it would be small, so there weren't a lot of things for Rachel to fret about. She had never been one of those little girls who wanted a big princess wedding or wanted to be the center of attention. She had never liked big crowds or parties, and it sounded like she was planning exactly the kind of wedding she wanted.

Faith didn't want to bring up the subject of Rick, but she knew she needed to ask if he would be there so she could prepare. Rachel beat her to it.

"Mom, I haven't wanted to bring this up because I didn't want to upset you, but I don't want you to be surprised ... I've invited Rick and his family to come to the wedding."

Her heart slammed into her throat. *Just keep yourself calm, Faith.*

"Okay. Thank you for warning me. I assume that means things are going well between you?" *Why did you ask that? You don't want to know!*

"Yes, we're getting to know each other. You'll be okay seeing him, right?"

"Yes, of course, Sweetheart. It's your day and I don't want you worrying about how he and I are doing. Everything will be fine."

Everything will be fine. She told herself that again as she hung up the phone.

The time had come to talk to Rick.

Chapter 25

N ow that he knew that he would be seeing Faith in a few weeks at the wedding, and probably earlier, he needed to take some action. The air needed to be cleared between them, and it needed to happen early enough that there was no tension at Rachel's wedding.

He had gotten some vague clues about Faith but still didn't have the whole picture — it was time to go to the source. Just as he was about to search online for her name again, his phone buzzed with a text from a number he didn't recognize.

"Rick, this is Faith. We need to talk."

His heart skipped a beat and breath caught when he saw her name on the text.

"I was just thinking the same thing. Name the time and I'll be there."

They quickly agreed on a time for a week and a half out and ended the conversation. He called Pastor Ray to see if they could use the church so they could talk in private. Rick and Faith both agreed not to mention it to Rachel so that she could focus on wedding preparations and not worry about them.

Rick went to the gym. Lifting weights would help him to focus while he thought about seeing her. A week and a half away seemed like an eternity, but Faith wouldn't be getting to Hideaway until then. He had a work trip to Asia anyway, so that would make a few of those days go faster.

He had very little idea of what to expect when he saw Faith. She looked so weak and out of it in all of the pictures he had seen at Rachel's. He had picked up on the fact that she hadn't lived in Hideaway for some time and that Rachel had, and had even gotten the idea that Rachel had probably lived with her grandmother for some time.

Had Faith struggled enough that she couldn't raise Rachel? What happened to the strong woman I knew? Did I break her?

He had talked to his friend Tim about Faith and the limited information he had about her. He told him about the shame he felt about changing her life in one night of impulse and about the night he thought about drinking when he was feeling that shame. Talking about his fears about sitting down with her had helped to calm him.

Tim encouraged him to spend some time confessing all of it to God and to confess to Faith and ask for her forgiveness when they met. He also reminded Rick that he needed to forgive her for not telling him about Rachel.

Rick wasn't sure how to do that. He felt like a jerk for ruining her life and felt sorry for her and for what had happened to her life since they knew each other, but he could not come up with one justification for her not telling him that he was a father.

Tim reminded him that God didn't see any justification for any of his behaviors and yet He had sent *His* child to die for him. It didn't turn sin into virtue; it simply set him free. When Rick forgave Faith, he would feel free, too.

Chapter 26

Faith looked around the lobby, taking in the place before leaving it for her new life. Many of the staff members and residents were there to see her off and pray for her travels and future.

Matt, the director, handed her his business card. "I know you have my information, but I'm handing this to you again today to remind you to keep me updated as you get closer to opening your own center. I'm here for consultation and encouragement anytime. If anyone can create another place like this, it's you."

Brandy hugged her again. "You're going to do great out there. You're ready."

"I'm going to miss you. Thank you, Brandy. I'll call you when I get settled in, okay?"

She took a deep breath and stepped through the door to her new life.

∞ ∞ ∞

When she arrived at the Ferrytown Motel the next day, she collapsed on the bed. Even with breaking up the drive with an overnight stop, the trip was tiring. It was good to have a couple of hours before Rachel and her mother were expecting her for dinner. She wanted to do some stretching and take a shower so that she could feel refreshed.

Her mother's suggestion that she stay at the Ferrytown instead of at Evelyn's so she would have more privacy was a good one. She wasn't introverted like her daughter, but she did need her alone time.

As usual she got ready early, so she took the long way to their house, making a quick pass by the lake. She breathed in as she looked at the still water and mounds of snow and continued on her way. The water always helped her to feel grounded, and she usually found reason to pass by it on her way anywhere she was going when she was in town.

When she walked up the steps to her mother's house, she wondered if she should knock or go right in. *What does Prodigal Child Etiquette dictate?*

Fortunately, her mother opened the door as she hit the top step. She opened her arms and any lingering fear she had about whether or not Grace wanted her there vanished.

"Welcome home, Faith." Rachel was right behind her grinning and followed with the same sentiment.

Faith was feeling very optimistic about her return to Hideaway.

Chapter 27

Rick arrived the day before his scheduled meeting with Faith so that weather wouldn't cause a delay. The conversation had been put off for long enough and he wasn't risking any more time.

He had made arrangements with Evelyn to rent a room for the three weeks leading up to the wedding and took some of his stockpiled vacation days so that he could just stay in town during that time. He was glad for the chance to be in one place for more than a few days, especially in the area that he was looking forward to spending a lot more time in. The B and B was a big step up from the cold hotels he was used to, and being there gave him the chance to get to know some of the people who were important to Rachel.

Now that he and Rachel had a relationship established and he would be visiting regularly, he was going to look into some more permanent accommodations in the area. He had found a used Jeep that would handle the winter roads well and had met a realtor at Rachel's church who had given him some leads on available properties in Summit County.

He was rarely in Chicago, so he just had a small, relatively cheap condo there. There was no reason to spend money on a place he wasn't in much and didn't care about.

He hoped to find a place, preferably on a lake, with room to have Rachel and Derek and their future kids visit, along with his family from Grand Rapids, and where he could ski and fish whenever he was in town during the summer. He was looking for a turnkey dream home and had made enough wise choices and investments with his money to be able to afford what he wanted.

The morning had been good for driving around looking at properties on Sapphire Lake, the inland lake he'd found so charming on his first visit to Summit County. Several of the properties were close to Lakes End, the tiny town where he had first come with Rachel and Derek for lunch. He was starting to get hungry and went to the Rock Creek Tavern, where they had eaten. It was empty except for a few tables and he didn't see anyone there to ask, so he found a table in the back and set to comparing his notes on properties.

He heard the waitress approaching and looked up.

"Welcome to the Rock Creek Tavern. My name is— *Rick.*"

"*Faith.*"

Chapter 28

I'm not sure I'm ready for this, Lord. I thought I had another day to prepare. She tried to be civil, but her contempt probably seeped through.

"So much for not having to see each other until tomorrow. What can I get you to drink?"

"Just water, please. It's good to see you, Faith." He gave a polite smile that completely threw her off.

Good to see me? How dare you.

She was so taken off guard that she couldn't even respond. She turned on her heel and walked straight back to the bathroom, figuring no one would notice or care if she just hid in there for a moment to gather her wits about her.

Her lightheadedness and racing heart were only because she was surprised and angry, or so she told herself. It didn't matter that he wasn't wearing a wedding ring or accompanied by a wife, or so she told herself.

She didn't care how good he looked with the little grey flecks in his hair or the five o'clock shadow that made him look like he'd just rolled out of bed. She would die before she would succumb to his charms again. What was underneath all of that was well-known to her and it was ugly.

"Lord, please do something here. I can't believe I have to *serve* him, of all things. He just waltzes in here saying it's *nice to see me?* It would have been nicer for him to see me while I was carrying his baby or trying to take care of a toddler with a broken back."

She reminded herself to breathe and talked herself through the moment as she looked at herself in the mirror.

"He's the man who left you and abandoned his child. He has no power over you, and whatever game he's playing, he's not going to win. You're back on your feet and you're not cowering."

When she had her bearings about her again, she took his water to him.

"You didn't poison it, did you?" He gave her his signature half smile, the one that used to send her head spinning.

If only I could.

She glared at him. "Let's save the small talk for tomorrow. Can I take your order?"

He lost the smile and his eyes clouded over. He spoke quietly and looked away. "It looks like I'm going to need a minute."

You're not the only one.

When she returned to take his order, he was gone and he had left another napkin with a note: "Faith, I'm sorry. I had no idea you were working here and I didn't mean to upset you. Hopefully we can start over when we meet tomorrow. R."

Cute, but the note-on-a-napkin trick only works once per lifetime.

Chapter 29

Rick kept his composure until he reached the sidewalk. He was glad to have the cold air and a gust of wind to counteract the heat on his cheeks. He also told himself that the heat was only anger.

She's going to act like I'm the bad one here? I thought we were going to be cordial and act like adults. Apparently she changed her mind.

He found another restaurant that looked like it was open and tried again. *I'm pretty sure no other women in Lakes End hate me, so this one should be safe.*

He was right — he was able to have a good meal and make notes about the homes he had looked at, especially the ones on Sapphire Lake. If he bought one of those, he could be close enough to Hideaway to see Rachel easily, but not so close that she would feel like he was invading her territory. He reminded himself that he wasn't in a rush to get something right away and that he could wait for the right place.

He was having a hard time concentrating on his task. His mind seemed to have its own ideas and kept wandering to Faith.

Faith. It was so strange to look into her eyes after so many years. She looked healthier than he expected after seeing the pictures of her and hearing the bits of information about the hard life she'd had, and she was even prettier than when she was younger. Her blonde hair was up away from her face, and he couldn't help remembering how he loved it like that in college because he could easily nuzzle her neck.

His emotions were a confusing, jumbled mess. He still struggled with guilt over changing the course of her life but was angry that *she* was angry. *How dare she keep my child from me and then act like I was the only one who messed up?*

Even in spite of the anger and guilt, he'd had to resist the urge to scoop her into his arms like he used to. He hated that there was even a hint of attraction toward her and reminded himself that she was not the girl he'd once loved.

He was not looking forward to tomorrow but he focused on his goal — there would be no scenes at Rachel's wedding.

He drove down by the beach and looked out over the water where the ice had formed enough to give a few brave — or possibly stupid — ice fishermen reason to haul their fishing shanties out. The last time he had been ice fishing was a few years ago, and he added it to the list in his head of things he would do as he began to put down roots here.

He wondered if Rachel liked fishing or skiing or any of the activities that he was looking forward to being a part of. It was still strange to have a daughter he knew so little about.

He closed his eyes and prayed. "Lord, thank You again for giving me the chance to know my daughter. Help me to keep learning about her and to find things to do with her. Help me find ways to be in her life and to be a good addition to it."

Swallowing hard, he prayed for the meeting with Faith. "Please take the anger that both of us feel away. Help me to forgive Faith for keeping Rachel from me and help her to forgive me for losing control with the girl I loved. Help us to both act like adults for the sake of our child." He prayed for every aspect of the meeting with Faith as if he was going through a pre-flight check of his instruments. It always calmed him to think about and hand over every detail of upcoming situations to God.

He prayed for protection of his heart as he pictured her in the restaurant. The haunted, numb, sad look he'd seen in the more recent pictures of her was replaced by fury and fire. The old line about women being beautiful when they were angry was certainly true in her case, but he warned himself of the consequences of falling for her again. She wasn't who he once thought she was and it definitely wasn't worth jeopardizing his relationship with Rachel.

He shook the thoughts away, asked God to take them and hide them from him, and headed back to Evelyn's.

Chapter 30

F aith was exhausted. Her first day at the restaurant had gone as well as she could have expected physically. She didn't have too much pain, but as she had promised herself she would do, she took an Epsom salt bath and sat against an ice pack as soon as she got back to the tiny motel room. She was all about preventing and being proactive these days.

While she was sitting still, she took the time to look for jobs and tried not to get discouraged when she found none. She was grateful that her old friend Chris had given her a job at the Rock Creek Tavern while one of his servers was in Florida for the winter, but she was hoping it would be a very short-term solution for his need for good help and hers for quick money.

The day would have been less exhausting if she hadn't had to have a run-in with Rick. *Rick.*

She still couldn't believe he just acted like they were old friends who happened to share a child and hadn't seen each other in years.

Nice to see me. Humph.

She had thought she had forgiven him, but his cavalier attitude got her blood boiling. *Did he just somehow forget that he left me high and dry? That he left* Rachel *high and dry?*

She hated the way she felt when she thought of him and tried

NEW BEGINNINGS IN SUMMIT COUNTY

to focus on what she wanted to say when they met. She saw at the restaurant that she needed an extra dose of willpower around him, both for the attraction and the fury. Having words and a strong focus for tomorrow would help her with that.

∞∞∞∞

The next day she woke up with a knot in her stomach. She did her exercises while her coffee was brewing and felt ready to focus when she sat down with her coffee, Bible, and journal. Thinking about Rachel and her wedding gave her a renewed determination to make things better, not worse, for her. She asked God to help her to keep the conversation focused on the wedding and to keep it brief.

She got to the church early and saw that she wasn't the only one. Rick looked like he was praying in his car, but she knew that couldn't be true.

She actually knew very little about him these days. There had only been the one conversation with Rachel about him, and the only thing she'd learned was that he lied and said he didn't know about Rachel.

It doesn't matter. All I need to know is that I'm not playing his game and that I'm laying down some ground rules for him today.

She saw him heading toward the front door of the church, so she purposely went in the back way. As much about this meeting as possible was going to be on her terms.

Chapter 31

P astor Ray showed Rick into the room where he'd first talked with Rachel, then retreated to his office. Rick was as nervous as he had been that day with Rachel, and after their interaction in the restaurant, he was on much higher alert for a slap coming in his direction.

Faith came in through the back door with her head high and jaw set. *She looks like she's planning her slap now.*

Despite her efforts to appear strong and secure, he noticed she still had the same tell of tucking her hair behind her ear when she was nervous that she'd had in college. He tried to forget how endearing he always found it to be and relaxed a little when he realized that she was as nervous as he was.

"Faith. Hi." He started to extend his hand, then thought better of it and gestured toward the chairs instead.

"Hello, Rick." The way she sat straight in the chair reminded him of a stern librarian.

She's as nervous as you are — she already showed you that.

"Sorry again about yesterday. I had no idea you were working there."

"It's fine."

He sat casually, hoping to put her at ease, and spoke first. "I'm glad you found my number. I was looking for yours too, and I'm glad we can talk."

Her eyes weren't quite glaring, but they weren't far off. "The only thing I want to talk with you about is Rachel's wedding and how we're going to make it a wonderful, perfect day for her. Any discussions about our past need to be off the table."

He focused on sounding agreeable. "Okay. Today is about Rachel. That discussion can wait." *But it will happen. I need answers.*

She seemed to catch his meaning, but stayed focused. "Fine. For now, we have wedding preparations and times when we have to be in the same room together over the next two weeks."

"I can play nice if you can, Faith." He kicked himself for letting some sarcasm creep into his tone.

She answered that with another glare. *So much for the weak-looking woman I saw in the pictures. When did sweet Faith turn so angry?*

"I've played nice when it came to you for twenty-five years, so yes, I can do it for two weeks."

What does that mean?

He reminded himself that they were there for Rachel and swallowed down the questions and the tirade in his head. He kept his tone as calm and cool as he could manage. "Okay, so from what I know about the festivities, the only times we have to be together are for the decorating, the rehearsal dinner, and the wedding. Let's just plan to stay on opposite sides of the room when we can and paste smiles on our faces when we can't."

"Agreed."

With that, she stood and walked away without looking back.

Leaving again. I suppose I should be used to her doing that by now.

As he walked out of the church, he was glad he had found a fitness center in town. He needed to release the tension that was taking over his entire body.

He couldn't stop thinking about what Faith had said. *How had she played nice for twenty-five years? Nice would have been letting a guy know that he was going to be a father.*

Chapter 32

Faith was relieved to have the meeting with Rick over but felt unsatisfied with how it had gone. She knew she had shut down most opportunities for conversation, but she had hoped he would override her long enough to apologize. The fact that he didn't only fueled the anger in her.

She was confused by the kindness she'd seen in his eyes when she first walked in and that fueled the fire too. He had looked at her as if he had nothing to apologize for and as if he actually cared.

Maybe he's a sociopath. I hope that's not genetic.

She pushed thoughts of him aside and focused on the day ahead. Rachel and Grace had invited her to go to church with them and they were meeting with the Coopers after for lunch.

Faith had always liked Derek and thought he was good for Rachel. Derek's father, Ed, had been a godsend when she had her accident, helping her navigate the ins and outs of the insurance issues and making sure she was taken care of. She still got a small monthly allowance from the settlement that helped her to live on her own and to get the treatments she needed, thanks to him.

It felt good to walk into the old church. She had always loved the place and remembered what an honor it was as a child to be allowed to ring the bells and light the candles for the service.

She had just gotten settled into her seat and started reading the bulletin when she heard a familiar deep voice behind her.

Rick. What in the world is he doing in church?

She pretended not to hear him and continued reading. Grace leaned over and warned her that he was there, and Faith thanked her and kept her eyes on the program.

"Are you going to be okay with him here?"

"I'm fine, Mom. Why is he here though? Is this to try to impress Rachel?" *I've seen this act before.*

The church bells sounded before Grace could answer and if there was one thing Grace Stevens didn't do, it was chitchat in church. Faith had to work hard to maintain her focus.

She was not surprised at all when Pastor Ray started talking about forgiveness. *I get it, Lord. I know. You know I'm trying, but having him show up every time I turn around is not making this any easier.*

Chapter 33

Rick was surprised to see Faith in church. He noticed her there just as he walked into the pew behind Rachel and sat as far down as he could to put space between himself and her.

I guess we're going to see if you can play nice today, Faith.

He was glad she was there even though it might make for an awkward service. From what he had gathered about her, she had strayed from the faith that had once inspired him. He hoped she was there because she had come back to it and not to impress Rachel.

He pretended to read the bulletin while he prayed that they would be able to form a truce and be cordial in front of Rachel. It felt like God was stirring up more prayers in his heart and he just kept going.

He prayed that they would be able to have a civil and honest conversation soon and that they would be able to clear the air. He prayed for her healing. He prayed for every activity associated with the wedding and handed each over to God. Finally, he asked God to help him to forgive her for the way she had acted since they had been reacquainted.

He chuckled at God's sense of humor when Pastor Ray started talking about forgiveness. God was certainly clever. He felt the nudge and promised Him that he would ask for Faith's forgiveness at his first opportunity.

The opportunity appeared more quickly than he had anticipated. At the end of the service, Grace turned to him and invited him to join them and Derek's family when they met them for lunch at the Birchwood Inn. It was obvious that she had talked to Faith about it first and Faith didn't look too happy.

As everyone else left the pews, Grace reached out a hand to both him and Faith. She gave them both a look that only mothers and grandmothers can give and 'suggested' that the two of them drive to the restaurant together so Faith could direct him.

He knew she was doing God's work and agreed. *Might as well get this apology over with. Please open her heart to accept it, Lord.*

He continued praying as he walked to his Jeep and pulled around to the entrance to pick Faith up. He glanced at Rachel and gave her what he hoped she would see as a reassuring look as he held the door open for Faith.

Faith avoided his gaze as she got into the passenger seat. *That's better than a glare.*

Chapter 34

Faith willed herself to use a kind tone. After all, she had just heard a sermon about forgiveness and promised God she was working on it.

"Sorry about my mother. You can just drop me off at the Ferrytown Motel on the way out of town and I'll drive my car over."

He returned the polite tone as he said, "I promised her I would deliver you safely to the restaurant and that's what I'm going to do. Plus, I need someone to tell me where it is. I'm new in town, you know."

She stared straight ahead so she didn't have to see the attempts at friendliness he was full of this morning.

Friendliness isn't all he's full of.

"Is that what you're doing? Moving here? How long are you going to keep up this Father of the Year bit, Rick?"

She bit her tongue but it was too late.

So much for being kind. I'm sorry, Lord.

Rick looked like he was going to react, then seemed to think better of it. "Faith, can we call a cease fire for just a few minutes? I promised God in there that I would say something to you and

I'm not in the habit of breaking promises to Him anymore."

Wait, what?

"Please?"

Faith nodded and looked ahead at the road as she tried again with the civil tone.

"Go ahead."

"I need to apologize — again. I know it's been twenty-six years, but I want to tell you again how sorry I am for not being stronger that night before I was deployed. It feels strange apologizing for something that resulted in the greatest gift I've ever received, but I want to say I'm sorry and ask for your forgiveness."

Faith was dumbfounded. She wanted desperately to be civil for Rachel's sake, but civility and pretense would have to wait until they got to the restaurant.

"What? *That's* what you want to apologize for? You've got to be kidding me. In case you've forgotten, you apologized for that immediately and I accepted it."

He looked like he was going to say something but she wasn't finished with him. "You're unbelievable. Do you think you can just change history and ride into town on your white stallion and be Rachel's father after twenty-five years?"

She couldn't help but glare at him again.

"Wait a minute, Faith. I'm trying to apologize to you and you're yelling at *me*? I kind of hoped that *you* might apologize for hiding my daughter from me for twenty-five years. How could you keep us apart?"

Now he was the one glaring.

"Nice try, but this is *me* you're talking to, Rick, not Rachel. I know you have her and everyone else fooled into thinking that you're some kind of victim here and didn't know about her, but we both know that's a bunch of bull. You need to stop this line and just be honest."

Rick looked like he had a death grip on the steering wheel and slowed down. "If I pull over for a minute, will you promise not to run away?"

"Well, since we're in the middle of nowhere and it's freezing out, I guess I don't have much of a choice."

He pulled over and stopped the car.

"What did you just say? What am *I* supposed to be honest about?" His eyes were full of fire now.

"You know. You always knew about her. You always knew and you left me to deal with the consequences of our actions. You left me to lie to her so she didn't know her father abandoned her. How could you leave me pregnant and alone, Rick? How could you leave *her!?* How could you reject your own child?"

She was fighting the tears, but losing, as twenty-six years of pain churned inside her.

"What do you mean, I knew and rejected her — or you? How could I know about her when you didn't tell me?"

She had never seen him this angry. She looked out the window to avoid his eyes.

"Faith? *How could I know!?*"

The tears were unstoppable now. The pain of remembering the empty mailbox was too much.

"Rick, *stop it*! In the letter I wrote you, I accepted your proposal and agreed to marry you when you came home on leave and told you I was pregnant. And then I never heard from you again." Her words were barely intelligible as she added, "I checked that mailbox every day looking for something — *anything*—from you."

"No." Rick shook his head and sat silently staring at the floor for a full minute.

He looked up at her with an intensity she had never seen.

His eyes were full of pain. The fear and despair she saw were very familiar — it was like the look she saw on that night so long ago, only worse.

"I never got a letter, Faith." His eyes were brimming with tears now, too.

She had seen men manufacture tears for her benefit and knew that was not what was happening — those were real and he was telling the truth.

Lord, no. Please tell me this is not what happened.

All she could do was cry.

He looked at her intently as his voice got quiet. "You really sent me a letter? All these years I thought you were so upset about what had happened that once I was out of the country, you were done with me."

He sighed as he ran his hands over his face. "I wanted to send you another letter when I didn't hear from you. I was so ashamed of tarnishing you, and my buddies kept telling me I was being a wuss and that instead of chasing you, I needed to just forget you."

She couldn't hide her pain at hearing he thought that of her. "You really thought I would just leave you?"

"And you thought I would just leave you." He looked as hurt by it as she felt.

They sat together, looking at each other, shocked and hurting and crying.

Faith had never felt as alone as she did sitting there. She wished he would reach over and hold her, but the days of him comforting her were long gone.

Chapter 35

Rick didn't know what to say or do. His gut told him she was being straight with him. *Could this be real?*

"Faith, please tell me what happened."

Just then, her phone rang. She gave an apologetic look as she showed him that it was Rachel calling and answered. It was obvious she was trying her hardest to act as if everything was fine for Rachel's benefit — it was also obvious that this wasn't the first time she'd done so.

"Hi, Sweetheart . . . No, we're not killing each other. We're just talking . . . I'm fine — we're both fine . . . Yes, I'm sure. We just needed to talk about something important. Go ahead and let them seat you and we'll be there in a few minutes."

She ended the call and looked at him. "Our daughter thinks she's my mother."

"Faith, can you tell me what happened before we have to go into a restaurant and paste smiles on our faces?"

"I got your letter the day after I found out I was pregnant."

No.

He felt like he'd been punched in the gut as he pictured the girl he left behind trying to absorb such news alone.

She wiped a tear from her eye. "I wrote back to you telling you that I loved you and wanted to marry you, too . . . and that I was pregnant and scared."

Rick couldn't help himself. He reached across the seat and pulled her close.

"I never got that letter, Faith. I would have gone AWOL to marry you if I had to. I'm so sorry you had to go through all of that alone."

She held onto him tightly. "How could this have happened?" Her voice broke.

"I don't know, honey. I don't know."

It felt so natural to hold her again that he almost forgot the circumstances. People were waiting for them and Rachel was worrying. "I really don't want to end this, but we should probably get this lunch over with and prove to Rachel that we didn't kill each other."

She almost laughed when she looked at him. "They'll think we tried if my eyes are as red as yours."

"They are, but that's okay. I'm glad we got this out and we can just fess up that we cried on each other's shoulders if anyone notices." He tried to give a comforting smile as he settled back into his seat.

"Rick, do you mind if we just wait here for a minute before heading over there? I really need to talk to God before I have to walk in there and be social."

Really? Oh, thank You, "So do I. Do you mind if I pray for us?"

He read the surprise on her face. "A lot of things have changed since you last knew me."

He reached out and took her hand as he bowed his head. "Lord, I think I can speak for Faith when I say that our heads are spinning right now. One thing I do know is that You are here for us and with us. Thank You for this conversation and for showing us what really happened, as painful as it is. Please help us to make sense of all of this and help us to walk into that restaurant and focus on Rachel and Derek and their special day. And, Lord, please heal Faith's wounds from all the years that she thought I had willingly abandoned her. I ask these things in Jesus' Name. Amen."

"Amen. Thank you, Rick."

He paused before putting the car in gear. "May I drive you home after lunch? This conversation doesn't feel over."

∞∞∞

Rachel looked nervous when they walked into the restaurant and more so when they approached the table and she saw their eyes.

Faith squeezed her shoulder and gave her a reassuring smile. "No blood, just tears. We're okay — we needed that conversation." Rick did his best to confirm what Faith said with a look and a nod.

The crowd had assumed they would want to be as far apart as possible and had left seats open at opposite ends of the table for them. The last thing he wanted to do was leave her side after the conversation in the car.

Rachel seemed to relax when she saw him hold Faith's chair out for her before finding his own seat. It seemed to serve as confirmation to her that they were truly okay.

Rick did his best to stay engaged in the conversation about wedding details at lunch, but all he wanted to do was get back in the car and hear the rest of the story from Faith.

Chapter 36

T he ride back toward Hideaway started in silence. Faith didn't know where to pick the conversation back up and she wondered if Rick was feeling the same.

He broke the silence. "I'm sorry I didn't try harder, Faith."

Her breath caught. "So am I, Rick."

"Do you feel up to talking more?"

"Yes, I would like that. I don't really have a place to entertain guests where I'm staying and you don't have privacy where you're staying, but I know a good place to talk in the car if you'd like to pick up some coffee and drive to it."

"Perfect."

∞∞∞∞

She directed him around the bay, through Shadow Hills, and up the winding road through the woods to the top of the hill overlooking Lake Michigan. They sat for a moment sipping coffee and looking down at the lighthouses that were covered in ice, making them look like glass creatures. The cold waves were hitting them and changing the shape of the creatures before their eyes.

She spoke first. "This is my go-to place when I need to contemplate or cry or be reminded of how big God is. I can't believe that as much time as you've spent here in the last month, no one has brought you up here."

"I can't either. It's beautiful — it's like the view from the plane. And it's nice to be in the same vicinity with you without you throwing darts at me with your eyes." He gave her a half smile as he said it, but she winced as she felt a stab of guilt for the way she'd treated him since she had arrived in town.

"Faith, I'm teasing. I'm surprised you weren't throwing real darts — or bullets — my way if you thought I had left you pregnant and alone and thought I abandoned Rachel." She could hear the sincerity as his voice cracked a bit. "I'm so sorry, Faith. I'm sorry I didn't write you a new letter every day until you agreed to marry me and I'm sorry I didn't come and find you when I was on leave . . . and I'm sorry that I believed you would just leave me."

It felt good to get the apology for what really happened and she hoped he would hear the sincerity in her voice too. "And I'm sorry that I didn't write you letters every day telling you to get home on leave and marry me before I got too big and round to walk down an aisle and I'm sorry I believed you would leave me too."

The tears took over again. "How did we get it so wrong?"

"I don't know."

They sat and stared at the waves for a long moment, until a thought occurred to Faith. "Wait a minute. If you thought I left you and hid Rachel from you all those years, why weren't *you* throwing darts at *me*? You were actually *nice* to me. Are you

116

really that good at forgiving?"

"Not even close," he laughed, "but I'm good at controlling my anger and I held it in until I was away from you. I took it out on gym equipment. I felt so much guilt over ruining your life that I didn't want to lash out at you." He paused, looking at her. "I don't know what happened, but I get the impression that your life got very hard. I'm sorry for the part I played in that."

She shook her head. "My life got very hard because when I was trying to be a good mom to a toddler and was trying to get home to her, some idiot was talking on a cell phone during a snowstorm on 75 and caused a nine-car pileup. I broke my back and a few other things, and up until several months ago, was in constant pain and hooked on narcotics. That's why my life eventually fell apart and why it got to the point where I couldn't raise Rachel." She felt overwhelming sadness again at what her life had turned into.

"Oh, Faith." He sighed as he rubbed his eyes and ran his fingers through his hair. "Neither of us got to raise our girl."

Chapter 37

Two days later, Rick arrived at Faith's room at the Ferry-town Motel right on time. "Good morning."

"Good morning."

She looked tired — it was no wonder. They had talked late into the night again last night as they tried to grasp the fact that they had both doubted and been doubted by the other. How it all could happen still perplexed them. They had both learned in their recovery groups about the importance of making amends and dealing with stress and heartbreak head on and had had some good, if painful, talks.

"Are you as tired as you look this morning?" She yawned even as she asked.

He gave a tired smile. "More. That's why the coffees waiting in the car are the biggest size they had."

"Perfect."

He offered his arm. "Ready for this?"

She nodded and took his arm as they walked in the slippery parking lot. The fresh blanket of snow was beautiful, but it made parking lots that were already uneven from previous snows treacherous. He walked slowly, not wanting her to get another back injury on his watch.

As she got in the car, she grabbed for the cup. "Thank you for the coffee. Ooh, and for warming the seat. This feels good. At least we don't have to be cold *and* tired."

"Are you sure you're up for this?" He didn't want her to push herself too much.

"Yes, this is the only time our schedules work together for the three of us to talk today. I don't want to put this off any longer."

"Me either."

They had asked Rachel if they could go to her place while Grace was at Bible study so they could have privacy as they filled her in on the full story of what transpired so long ago. They wanted to tell her as soon as possible so that she would stop worrying about why they both had looked so shaken at lunch on Sunday. Each of them had tried to assure her that everything was fine and they had made peace with each other, but she wasn't satisfied.

She still looked concerned when she opened the door. "Good morning."

Rick tried to keep it light as they walked through the door. "Tea for the lady."

"Thank you. I'm glad you could both come before I have to work. Can we sit down in the living room and talk before we have breakfast?"

"Of course, Sweetheart." Faith put her arm around Rachel as they walked into the living room.

Faith and Rick sat on either side of Rachel on the couch as Faith began, "I'm sorry to have worried you and I know that it's my fault that you think you have to mother me, but you don't have to do that anymore."

Rachel listened quietly as Faith continued. "What you saw the other day was the aftermath of the most painful conversation I've ever had, but also probably the most important. I found out that what I had believed about Rick for twenty-six years was wrong."

Faith looked at Rick as if to encourage him to step in.

He set his coffee down and put his hand on Rachel's arm. "And I found out that what I believed about your mother since the moment I found out about you was wrong, too."

They told her the whole story in tandem. Rachel listened intently as they told her about how they each thought the other had left them and how horrible they each felt for doubting the other. They all shed tears as they talked about the tragedy that had befallen their family.

"I think I can speak for your mother when I tell you how sorry we both are for giving up on each other. We both gave away the family you should have had — we all should have had together — because we were afraid." He looked into Rachel's eyes. "I'm sorry, Rachel. I'm sorry that I wasn't man enough to chase down the woman I loved and that I wasn't here for you for your whole life. I hope you will forgive me and give me the chance to make it up to you."

"Of course I forgive you. I gave up on Derek once and it's the biggest regret of my life, just like having his forgiveness is the biggest gift of my life. I don't judge you for doing what I did."

She suddenly got a look of confusion on her face and looked at Faith. "But Mom, you said you didn't tell him about me in your letter to him."

Faith looked down as the tears started filling her eyes again. "I'm sorry, Sweetheart. I asked God to forgive me even as I lied to you. I promised myself that I would never tell you that your father abandoned you. I didn't want you to carry that around. Now that I know he didn't, I'm glad I kept it from you."

She looked up at Rick with sorrow in her eyes and reached for his hand. "I'm so sorry I believed that about you."

He had his own tears in his eyes. "I know, Faith." He pulled them both into a family group hug that turned into a family group prayer as they asked God to heal all that was broken.

∞∞∞∞

As they drove away from Rachel's house, Rick felt like a weight was off his chest. "Do you feel as relieved as I do after that?"

"Definitely. Now that there aren't any mysteries or grudges or bitterness, we can all move forward." She laughed and added, "We're a strange little family, aren't we?"

"That we are."

He started driving back around the bay to go up to the overlook where they had spent so much time over the past few days.

"Back up the bluff again . . . good idea."

"I agree with you that it's a great place to be reminded of how big God is. If there was ever a time when we needed God to be big, this is it."

After he parked the car, he turned to her. "When we were telling the story to Rachel, I realized something. I'm done with being upset or hurt that you didn't believe in me — I'm over it. I'm having a much harder time letting go of the fact that *I* didn't believe in *you* and I may beat myself up for that one for the rest of my days. But as far as you doubting me is concerned, I'm done. I know you feel as awful as I do and I forgave you and I'm glad we're friends again."

She gave a small smile as she answered. "And I'm done, too . . . 'as far as the east is from the west,' right? What's done is done and we've apologized and forgiven. And I'm glad we're friends again, too. I think we'll always carry the scars from giving up on each other but we can help each other to not dwell on it."

She took a breath and continued. "So, in the spirit of moving on from that and changing the subject, why didn't you ever marry? I assumed that you'd show up in town with your beautiful wife and kids and dog and perfect family for Rachel to join into."

Rick answered honestly. "There was only one person I ever wanted that with."

The honesty got to be a little too much. He swallowed hard and looked down the coast. "After you, I took a long break from women. When I did start again, I dated a few women for long stretches, but the relationships were always on the back burner for both of us. I focused on my career, first in the Air Force and then with the airline. I could control that — I set goals and met them. They didn't depend on anyone else sticking around or feeling a certain way. It was all on me." The illusion of control had been a good friend to him.

"I dated women who were as career focused and busy as I was, and it worked well, or so I thought. The last relationship I was in went on for six years, until she had had it with my drinking. She threatened to go to the airline if I didn't take care of it even though I never drank before a flight." Faith's smile conveyed understanding as she listened.

"Trina saw the warning signs that we had both seen in others and I was ignoring in myself. I took a long, hard look at the life I was living and person I was on the verge of becoming, stopped drinking, found God, got more serious about school, and got my life back on the right track."

He smiled as he turned to her. "And then at twelve-thirty a.m. on Christmas morning, I got an email saying that I was a father and the greatest adventure of my life started." It was still hard to believe that he was a father and that he was sitting and sharing his story with Faith. "What about you? Did you ever date, or did the accident throw you so off course that it took over your whole life?"

She looked down and he hoped he hadn't hit a raw nerve. "Well, after I finally accepted that you weren't coming back, I gave in to friends who kept trying to set me up. I went on a few dates, but at that age, the men weren't looking for a package deal, and once they found out I had a child, that was it. And I was doing the same thing you were in different ways. I didn't want to get dumped and get my heart ripped out again either. "

She gazed out at the lighthouses. "After the accident *everything* changed. Eventually as I grew more addicted and hopeless, I settled for men who didn't treat me well and weren't good for Rachel. When men cheated and lied, I rationalized it because at least they weren't abusing either of us. I wanted so badly to give Rachel a family that I held onto bad relationships hoping they would get better — they didn't. *Shocker*."

How any man could treat Faith that way was incomprehensible to him. He shoved his thoughts aside and listened.

"I was a shell of myself and lived in denial. Eventually, my mother stepped in and asked if she could take Rachel. In my greatest moment of clarity, I agreed. I knew I was damaging her and didn't know what else to do to save her."

That act must have taken all of her strength.

The same strength seemed to propel her to continue. "When she was gone, I had no compass anymore and spiraled down. It was like I was determined to show God that if He could turn His back on me, I could turn my back on Him. I turned my back on Him and on myself and on Rachel at that point." She shuddered.

"Thankfully, even though I had turned my back on God, He hadn't turned His on me. He used the lure of physical rehabilitation to get me to Healing Rock and He met me there."

She finally turned back and met his gaze. "And to bring it around to now, that's why as bewildered and heartbroken as I am for all that we lost, I can't turn my back on Him again. I *won't*. I have to believe there was a reason for all that loss and heartache and I have to believe that He will bring good out of it."

Once again, he couldn't help himself and reached across to hold her. "I have to believe that, too. He's brought both of us back into Rachel's life and that's what matters now. He'll use all of it."

He realized he was liking the hug a little too much and drew back.

Maybe someday. Not now.

Chapter 38

Faith didn't want him to stop hugging her when he pulled away. *This isn't twenty-six years ago and this isn't the time. Change the subject.*

"One thing that I know for sure that He's brought out of all of the misery I went through is that He's given me a desire to start a treatment center. I want to help other people who have had the same struggles I had someday."

He smiled. "I can see you doing that. It's a great idea and you know it's needed. What are you planning to do?"

Faith felt so comfortable talking with him that she decided to let him in on her plans. "I'd like to start a place like Healing Rock. I worked in the office there so I had the inside understanding of what it took to run it. Part of my job was knowing the history, structure, and mission well enough to communicate it to potential donors and referral sources, so I had a great opportunity to study everything and see how to duplicate what they've created. Every night I took notes of what I had learned through the day, so I have a big, thick folder with ideas. My hobby for the past several months has been making drafts of policies and procedures and business plans."

He started laughing and Faith felt her spirits fall.

He must have read the look on her face, because he immediately put his hands up and said, "No, I'm not laughing at your idea or plans. They're great and you're going to do it. I'm laughing because it just so happens that the name of one of my classes this semester is literally *Business Planning*, so I guess both of us spend our free time developing business plans."

"Really?"

"Really. I enjoy it because I have some ideas for future businesses, but it's obvious by the look on your face when you talk about it that it's more fun for you than for me. When it's a passion project, it's a whole different ball game. What can I do to help?"

She tried to temper her excitement. "Well, it's a bit off in the future, but I might take you up on that offer someday. Right now it's still in the dream stage."

He seemed excited about it, too. "Just let me know. I don't know what would have happened to me if I hadn't walked into the first recovery meeting. God used Trina's threat to report me to get me through the door. He'll use your center for others just like he used that church for me and Healing Rock for you."

Chapter 39

Rick had more houses to look at on the lake and when he finished, he went to the Rock Creek Tavern for the third lunch of the week. It was nice to talk to Faith and not worry about his water being poisoned.

She smiled when she saw him. *Much better than the glare.*

"I'm due for a break if you would like some company for lunch."

He smiled at her. "I may have come here this late hoping that was a possibility."

It was great to have the air clear with her and to have their friendship back. They had seen each other each day since the big conversation on Sunday and he was starting to get used to it.

He wanted to pick the romance back up and suspected that Faith was feeling the same way, but so much water had passed under the bridge that neither of them were ready to enter into a new relationship lightly.

They also had Rachel to consider. Even though the circumstances were very different, they were both forming new relationships with their daughter and both were determined to make sure nothing got in the way with her.

He had more conversations with God than anyone over those

KATHERINE KARROL

four days and had even gone and talked with Pastor Ray. He knew the pastor had gone through loss and he trusted his input.

Pastor Ray told him about his own anger at God when his first wife died, and he assured Rick that God was not threatened by his strong emotions. He encouraged him to keep having the honest conversations with God and letting Him do His work in Rick's heart. Rick could see that Pastor Ray was not holding grudges with God or still swimming in grief, and it gave him hope.

Faith sat across from him with the same overflowing bowl of salad she'd had every time she ate with him there.

"Don't you ever get sick of eating the same thing every day?"

She pointed to her back with her fork. "Inflammation is not my friend, remember? This is the only quick thing on the menu that won't make this worse. I'm already pushing it doing a job that requires me to be on my feet for hours."

She grinned as she dug into the salad. "How's the dream house hunting coming along?"

"It's coming. There are some great properties, but none are turnkey. I may have to settle for getting something that needs some work. It doesn't have to be perfect, but I want to be able to move in as soon as possible. Staying at Evelyn's is great for now, but since I'm going to be coming up here regularly, I need my own space."

She reached across the table and picked up one of the print-outs he had been looking at. "Wow, look at the beach that comes with this one."

"Look at all the other work that needs to be done, though. I want simple. Okay, maybe I want perfect." He chuckled as he changed the subject. "Speaking of projects, I want to hear more

127

about your dream treatment center. I haven't been able to stop thinking about it since you told me about it the other day."

"Well, since it's pretty far off in the future, all I can do for the moment is make lists of what I want to be a part of it and work on the business plan." She shrugged and focused on his printouts.

"Faith, let me help you with the business plan. Please? I have to make three more of them just for the one class this semester, so it would be helping me, too. Help a poor college student out." He made praying hands and gave his best attempt at puppy dog eyes.

She looked at him teasingly. "Are you asking if you can be my intern?"

He laughed. "I will get you all the coffee you need and make as many copies as you ask for. Seriously, though, can I look at the plans? The sooner you have the business plan set, the sooner you can file paperwork and start fundraising, and the sooner you can get paid to do what you're already doing. This center is going to help so many people."

His excitement for her project was rising. "Faith, I knew so many people in my recovery group whose opiate addictions started when they had injuries. A couple of them lost their families and jobs and reputations because the addiction took over their lives. This center is going to help people like them and people like you. And I hate to pull this card, but this center is going to help people like Rachel who are losing their parents to addiction and pain . . . Faith, what are you waiting for?"

She pushed her empty bowl away. "You're right. I've had this idea that I needed to have more time under my belt of being clean and healthy. Maybe I need to adjust my timeline."

As she stood up from the table, she said, "Okay, intern. I have to go back to work, but your first assignment is to find us a place to look at the business plan. Your car is great for talking but doesn't make for a very good workspace. I have papers to spread out and need room. If you succeed at that assignment, I'll let you drive me around and you can see the properties I've been looking at."

He gave her a salute. "Yes, ma'am."

Chapter 40

Faith was nervous about showing her plans to Rick. It was strange to think that five days earlier she hated being in the same room as him and today she was showing him the plans for her dream.

Since Evelyn would be at book club and the others who lived there were out of the house for the morning, Rick had invited her to come over there and use Evelyn's large dining room table to go over her materials.

It was comforting to be in Evelyn's home again. It had been a few years and she had loved the place since she was a child. Evelyn and her mother were very close, and Evelyn had always been like an aunt to Faith.

When she arrived, Rick met her at the door with a cup of coffee and took her tote bag. "Good morning, boss. Can I get you any copies today?"

She playfully hit his arm with her free hand as they walked into the dining room. "Watch it, intern, or I'll have you collating and sorting paper clips."

His eyes got big as she started pulling folders out of her bag. "I organized the one big folder so that we could make sense of it today."

"Hey, I thought I was the intern. You're doing my job?"

"I'm trying to make your job easier so we can accomplish more than sorting today."

She held some of the files close to her chest for a moment and took a deep breath. "Rick, this feels scary showing you this stuff, so go easy on me, okay?"

His eyes grew serious as he stretched his hand out toward the folders. "Of course. This is your calling and your future. I'll handle it with care, I promise."

She showed him the draft of the business plan that she felt most confident with and held her breath as he started looking it over. He seemed engrossed in it, and she studied him as she tried to gauge his response. When she realized that her eyes had wandered to the muscles on his arms, she focused instead on her coffee cup.

He looked up at her as he finished. "Faith, this is really good. I mean, *really* good. Are you sure you haven't been taking business classes?"

She allowed herself to hope that her dream could happen.

He slid his notepad over to her. "Look. I made those notes last night about what needed to be in your plan as I was thinking about what you've told me so far about this place. You hit every one of the items on this list and then some."

She felt a mix of relief and pride and a sudden impatience to get things going and make the dream a reality. "Great job, intern. Your next task is to be my chauffeur so I can show you the properties I've found for this. Let's go."

Faith returned to Evelyn's the next afternoon for Rachel's bridal tea. It was hard to believe that her little girl was getting married in a week.

It was the first time Faith was seeing some old friends and acquaintances since her return to Hideaway, and she was looking forward to catching up. When she arrived, Shelby, Evelyn, Grace, and the ladies from Grace's Bible study and various clubs were scurrying around making everything perfect. After all the hugs, congratulations, and assurances of their continued prayers, Faith joined them in putting the final touches on the décor and food.

Emily Spencer, Evelyn's boarder and a new friend of Rachel's, was helping as well. They had met briefly at church and she knew Emily was dating Joe Callahan, Brianna's brother, but they hadn't had a real conversation.

They had some time to talk while they arranged the fruit tray in the kitchen, and when Faith found out that Emily was an accountant, she told her about her plans to start the treatment center and the business plan that she and Rick had been working on. Emily seemed excited about the idea and offered to look over the budget Faith was working on for it. Emily shared that she had started a new life in Hideaway and said she would be thrilled to have a small part in others getting a new chance as well.

Rick had flown down to Kingsville to pick up his mother, sister, and niece, and Faith was feeling nervous about meeting them. She reminded herself that he had assured her that they didn't blame her for anything when he told them what had happened. She knew they had immediately fallen in love with Rachel and hoped she could make a good impression as well.

Rachel looked beautiful when she arrived with Brianna in tow and Faith couldn't imagine how beautiful she would be as a bride. She would find out soon.

Chapter 41

Rick felt a surge of pride as he made a large circle over Hideaway and Lakes End to show off some of his favorite sights before landing. He pointed out the homes on Sapphire Lake that he had looked at with the realtor and all were met with approval.

Everything had a fresh blanket of snow, so it looked crisp and new. Lake Michigan and Sapphire Lake even displayed extra vivid colors for the guests. He pointed out more sights on the short drive from the airport to the Shoreside Inn, and his family was happy about the roots he was putting down and new life he was creating.

They were all taken with Evelyn's home, as he had been. Both his mother and sister had a special fondness for Victorian homes and antiques, so he knew they would love the place. They would be staying there when they came for the wedding, and he was looking forward to having more time then to show them around.

Today, though, he truly felt like a proud father as he ushered them into the parlor where Rachel was surrounded by the women who loved her most. She looked beautiful in a light pink dress and was smiling like a very contented bride.

Of course his eye was immediately caught by Faith, and when she saw him, she and Grace made their way over to meet his family. He shot up a quick prayer for Faith's peace when he saw her nervous tell as she approached.

His mother and Debbie both hugged Faith and Grace as if they'd known them for years. He could see the relief on Faith's face and he couldn't resist a quiet "I told you so" and a wink when she came close enough to hear it.

Faith looked like she was as mesmerized by Rachel as he was as she spoke. "Can you believe that we, the mother she barely had contact with and the father she didn't know two months ago, are standing here together watching our daughter, the bride-to-be? This doesn't seem real."

Faith's eyes were misty as she said it, and Rick instinctively put his arm around her and kissed her on her temple.

"No, it doesn't seem real." *It sure seems right, though.*

He cleared his throat and said, "Well, you ladies have a nice time. I'm off to join the men on the ski slopes."

"Just keep my future son-in-law in one piece. No big jumps on Summit Mountain today."

He looked back just in time to see his sister giving him a smirk. *She's way too perceptive.*

He gave her a 'who, me?' shrug and was out the door.

Chapter 42

By the time Faith met with Rachel to go to her final dress fitting, she had already had a productive morning. It felt great to get things accomplished before lunchtime rolled around like she used to in the old days.

She enjoyed the moment as she waited for Rachel to come out of the fitting room. *It's good to be among the living again.*

As promised, Emily had sat down with her earlier in the morning and looked over the budget she had begun drafting. Emily was impressed with the detail that was there and said that Faith was further along on it than she realized. She promised to look over the numbers and to make sure it was solid so that Faith could start the fundraising.

Emily was excited about the project and seemed to understand the mission and dream, so Faith asked her to join the board. She enthusiastically accepted the invitation, but before they could discuss the details further, Joe Callahan and his daughter Lily came through the front door. It warmed Faith's heart to see how little Lily ran to Emily as soon as she saw her and to see how happy Joe was. Joe had been devastated when his first wife died suddenly and it was good to see that he was getting a second chance at happiness with Emily. Faith suspected it wouldn't be long before Emily's mother would be sitting in the seat Faith was in waiting to see *her* daughter in a wedding dress.

When Faith and Emily filled Joe in on what they were working on, he volunteered to help with any renovation needs they would have once they found a place to house the center. When Faith left there that morning, she had some extra air in her step as she saw her dream coming together.

When Rachel walked out of the fitting room in her wedding dress, Faith felt her eyes mist up. "Oh, Sweetheart, you look beautiful. I'm so happy for you."

Rachel had her moment, too, when she looked in the mirror. "I'm trying to focus on how great it is to be doing this now instead of how we should have been doing this two years ago."

Faith put her arms around her daughter and met her eyes in the mirror. "Oh, Rachel. I know things didn't work out the way or in the timing that you planned before, but I see how he looks at you and how the two of you are together. You have something very special."

She took a deep breath to keep the tears in check. "You know, you and I are in the same boat here. We've both been extended grace, you from Derek and me from you and Grandma and even Rick. We both need to allow God to wash away the shame and the guilt for past mistakes and accept the gift of new chances we've been given. I'll help you and you help me, okay?"

"Okay, Mom. You're right. I'm so glad you're able to be a part of this." Rachel turned and hugged her tightly like she used to as a little girl. "The one thing that is great about this happening now instead of two years ago is that you and Rick are both here. I'm so happy to really have you back again."

It felt like everything was falling into place. She had a better relationship with Rachel and her mother than she could have imagined after all the years in the fog, she was managing the physical discomfort well enough to lead a normal life, she was making steps with the treatment center, and she had a good friendship again with Rick.

She often had to repeat the verse about taking every thought captive when it came to him, but she forced herself to put any thoughts of anything other than friendship and sharing a daughter on the shelf. Nothing was going to threaten her relationship with Rachel, even fairy tales in her head about reuniting with the great love of her life.

Chapter 43

Rick was glad he'd taken the vacation time he had so that he could be a part of all of the wedding preparations. He liked to be helpful, and it gave him a great chance to get to know the new people in his life.

He and Derek were careful as they hauled the arbor Derek had made out of birch branches up the stairs of the church and into the sanctuary.

"You know you're putting all of your friends to shame with this, right, Derek? Most guys think the only thing they need to do for their weddings is show up."

"Most guys don't get to marry Rachel." Derek's smile showed that he was as in love with Rachel as a man could be.

"Good answer, son." Rick decided to take the opportunity while they were alone for a moment to get fatherly. "I know I've only been in Rachel's life for a short time, but I want you to know how happy I am that she's marrying you. I could see something special between the two of you from the day we met, and as I get to know her I can't imagine anyone more suited for her than you."

"Thank you, sir. There's no one more suited for me than her, either. I spent three and a half years without her and I was a miserable mess." He adjusted the arbor to center it. "I'm glad she's got you, too. I didn't know what to expect when we found out about you, but you've been just what she needed in a father."

Rick smiled at that. "Even one who's late to the party?"

Derek shrugged. "Better late than never. She always wanted a family, and now she's got you and a whole new set of family members, and even her mom back. I don't think she could ask for anything more right now."

"You're right."

Neither of them had noticed Rachel walk into the sanctuary.

"I've got everything I've ever wanted." She had a big smile on her face as she looked at them, then the arbor. She turned to Derek and said, "Do you mind if I have a minute with my dad?"

Rick's breath caught. *Did she just say 'dad'?*

She waited for Derek to exit the sanctuary before speaking. "Rick, when Derek and I got engaged, his father offered to walk me down the aisle and I gladly accepted the offer. Even during the years that Derek and I were apart, Ed was very sweet to me and still treated me like family. In many ways, he was the closest thing I ever had to a father."

"That's wonderful, Rachel. I'm glad he was there for you when I couldn't be." *Thank You, God, for putting decent men in her life when I wasn't here.*

"He asked me last night if I would rather have you walk me down the aisle, and I told him I would." She looked at him shyly. "Will you walk me down the aisle tomorrow?"

He scooped her into a bear hug and spun her around. "Really, Rachel? *Of course* I will. You've made me the happiest man around today — well, apart from your groom."

Thank You, God. I get to have a Dad job at my daughter's wedding.

Chapter 44

Rachel is getting married today. Faith felt pure happiness as she woke up in her childhood bedroom.

She spent time thanking God for giving Rachel a good man who treasured her and for being able to be a part of Rachel's special day. She was especially grateful that Rachel had asked her to be a part of the slumber party at her house the night before her wedding. She was not surprised that Shelby and Brianna were staying the night but being included too surprised and thrilled her.

She was just as surprised and thrilled the day before when Rachel asked her to walk her down the aisle along with Rick. She thought of the irony that the first thing they would be doing together publicly as her parents would be walking her down a wedding aisle.

After the rehearsal dinner, Rachel pulled Faith and Rick aside and told them that she didn't want any secrets between her and them before her wedding and told them that she had a secret career as a writer. She gave them each copies of her most recent book, which was the only one she had written under her real name instead of a pseudonym and was the one she was most proud of. The cover art was beautiful, and she beamed as she told them that Derek had painted it after reading the book. She was far more comfortable gushing about the cover than the book, and Faith knew that it took a lot for Rachel to feel at ease sharing it with them.

Faith couldn't have been more proud or grateful. For the first time since she allowed Rachel to go live with her mother, Faith felt like she had a place in her life.

∞∞∞

"Rachel, I don't even know what to say. You're stunning, Sweetheart."

Rachel glowed in the simple and elegant white dress, and the way the veil framed her face made her look like an angel. "Thanks, Mom. I'm so glad you're here."

Rick walked in and Faith's heart almost stopped.

Lord, how am I supposed to only see him as a friend and as Rachel's father when he shows up in a tux looking like that?

Their eyes met and she felt her cheeks warm when she saw how he looked at her.

Take every thought captive, just friends, take every thought captive, just Rachel's father ...

"Wow, Rachel, you're the most beautiful bride I've ever seen." His voice caught as he looked at his daughter. "I'm not sure I'm worthy to be walking down the aisle with two such beautiful ladies."

Faith couldn't help but picture the wedding that should have happened twenty-six years ago, with the man in front of her before the gray dotted his hair and the lines formed into his face. He was even more handsome now than he had been then.

Take every thought captive.

She forced herself to focus on the present. Today was Rachel's wedding and they were walking her down the aisle to start her new life with the man of her dreams.

After Rick stepped back out of the room, Rachel turned to her. "Mom, what are you doing?"

"What do you mean?"

Rachel gave her a look. "I see what's going on between the two of you. You've been practically inseparable since you found out about the missing letter and forgave each other. Why are you fighting what you know you both want?"

"We're both focused on you right now. We've both lived whole lives apart and had our difficulties. We're friends and he's your father. That's it, at least for now."

"Mom, do you believe what he says and who he presents himself to be? I do, and I think you do too, or you would be trying to keep him away from me. I lost three and a half years with Derek and I wish with everything in me that I had every minute of them back. You lost twenty-six years with Rick — do you really want to lose more time?"

Before Faith could answer, Rachel walked toward the door.

"Let's go. I'm two years late in marrying Derek, and I don't want to wait a minute longer."

Chapter 45

Rick stood back, watching the scene in front of him. As Rachel danced with her new husband, she looked like the happiest woman in the world. They went back and forth between staring into each other's eyes and giggling.

He couldn't imagine a better feeling than this.

Debbie appeared at his side. "Having fun, Smiley?"

"This is quite possibly the best night of my life." He draped his arm around her and kissed her on the cheek. "I'm so glad you're here for this."

"Me too. I couldn't help but notice that you've hardly been able to take your eyes off the mother of the bride all day. What are you going to do about her?"

"What do you mean, what am I going to do about her?"

"I've seen you with every girlfriend you've ever had and I've seen the way you were with them. This look," she did a circle around his face with her hand, "is only for Faith."

He couldn't help but smile. "We're both focusing on building our respective relationships with our daughter right now. Maybe someday, but not now."

"Ricky, look at that blushing bride on the dance floor. She

doesn't even know you exist right now. You thought you had *someday* with Faith twenty-six years ago. Don't make the same mistake twice."

He gave her a squeeze. "You're pretty smart for a little sister."

With that, he strode across the room directly to Faith. He bowed and extended his hand to her. "May I have this dance?"

She looked flustered and blushed as she took his hand and let him lead her to the dance floor.

When he drew her close, she didn't resist. He could hold her in his arms forever if she would let him.

He looked into the face he had been haunted by for over half of his life. "Faith, I lost out on twenty-six years with you and twenty-five with Rachel because I was afraid of getting shot down and looking like a wuss. I'm afraid of making our daughter uncomfortable if it doesn't work out, but I'm even more afraid of losing you again if I don't take the chance."

He gently brushed a stray hair from her cheek as he spoke. "Will you take a chance with me?"

She grinned up at him. "Yes, I will. I've been trying to fight the feelings I've had, too, but I don't want to risk losing you again, either. *No letters* this time, though."

She laughed and held him tighter, and it was as if he was taken back in time to the college dance floors where he first learned to move with her like this. They moved together easily, cheek to cheek.

When he glanced up, he saw Rachel smiling in their direction.

Best night of my life.

Chapter 46

Faith put the last sweater in the drawer and looked around the bedroom, satisfied. *One thing about living a transient lifestyle, it doesn't take long to move in somewhere.*

It was strange to look around her childhood bedroom and think that it was her new home. She was surprised when Grace suggested she move in there and was going to turn the offer down, but Rick pointed out that if she paid the reasonable rent Grace was offering, she wouldn't have to take extra shifts that took a toll on her back.

She also recognized that it was confirmation that Grace saw that she really was back on her feet. For most people, moving back into their parents' home would be a step backward — for Faith, it was proof of steps forward. It was a good solution for both of them financially and they had agreed that they would reevaluate after a month and decide if the arrangement was working or not.

Rick brought in the box of books and set it on her desk. He looked around the room and smirked. "I probably shouldn't be in here, should I?"

She laughed. "Just stay on that side of the room and we'll be fine."

"I have a better idea. Come on."

∞∞∞

Riding in the plane next to Rick gave Faith a special kind of thrill. He maneuvered the little Cessna with the skill of the pro that he was, but the look on his face as he did so was almost childlike joy. Between watching him and watching her home-town below, Faith was overwhelmed by the sights before her.

"I can't believe this is your view from the office, Rick. This is amazing — talk about being reminded of how big God is."

"You see why it's my favorite part of my job. Seeing mountains and deserts and areas like this from a God's-eye view never gets old. Views like this have made the drudgery of living half my life in hotel rooms worth it. I can't believe you've never had the chance to see Summit County from this angle."

"It's even better getting to see it with my intern as my pilot — since I'm your boss, I get to tell you where to go."

They laughed together, but she saw a smirk on his face and felt like she was missing out on an inside joke. Suddenly she realized that he had been circling the plane for a few minutes.

"Rick, why are we circling the Rowland farm?"

"Because out of all of the properties that you've pointed out as potential sites for the treatment center, *that*," he pointed down, "is the one that you get the most excited over."

"I do love it and it would really be perfect. But why are we here? It's going to take months of fundraising before I can even consider putting in an offer on a property."

He pulled an envelope wrapped in a napkin out of his pocket.

She laughed when she saw that there was writing on the napkin. "You and your napkin stationery."

"It worked the first time."

"Yes, but the second time, I used it to clean gum off the bottom of a table."

He laughed and his eyes twinkled. "Well, let's hope the third time is lucky. Read it and tell me what you think."

Faith only got partway through it. "Rick, no. You can't do this."

"I can and I want to. Will you please let me?"

"You want to take out the mortgage for the center in your name?"

"Read further. The mortgage would be in my name, but the property would be in the center's."

"Rick, this is a lot of money."

"Consider it back child support."

She couldn't help but laugh — he chuckled too. "Too soon?"

She looked back at the document in her hand. "You really want to do this? You've been looking at dream homes on Sapphire Lake for weeks — you can't do both."

"You're not the only one who has had budget strategy sessions with Emily. She's confirmed the numbers I've come up with and I can do both, with some adjustments." His jaw was set in determination. "I had been thinking about leaving the airline, but I'll stay on for a while longer. Thanks to my seniority, I make my work schedule and can time trips so that I only work eleven or twelve days a month. It leaves me plenty of time to be here and it makes me a good living that gives us options."

Us?

"If I buy this property, or any other property you would prefer, and donate it to the center, it offsets the sale of my condo in Chicago. Selling that frees up money to get my house on the lake. Instead of getting one that someone else has done the work on, I'll get one that needs a little bit of attention. It will save a lot of money and give me something to do when I'm not wooing you or helping you at the center or pressuring our daughter to make me a grandpa. I've already talked to Joe about overseeing the plans and doing the work that I can't do."

She tried to absorb all that he had just said. "Wow, you've been giving this a lot of thought. Wait, you're going to sell your condo in Chicago? Does that mean—?" She was afraid to be too hopeful.

He looked intently into her eyes. "I don't want to be there any more than I have to when my family is here. I want to make a go of this, Faith. I want to make a go of being in Rachel's life for more than occasional visits and help at the center and put down roots and be part of a community. And I *really* want to make a go of *us*. I've been in commuter relationships and they were perfect for me then because I wasn't all in. I'm all in with you. I'm trying to make up for twenty-six years of lost time and I can't do that living in another state."

She threw him a coy look. "You haven't even kissed me yet and you're going to move for me?"

The flash in his eyes when she said it set her insides on fire.

He let out a groan and rubbed his face with his hand. "You have no idea how hard that has been — it's taken every bit of my self-control. I'm going to protect your honor this time, and if I have to stay away from you to limit temptation, I'm going to. We're doing it right this time."

When he took her hand in his and kissed it, her stomach did a flip.

She smiled at him. "I appreciate that. I don't want to risk too much temptation either. I guess we'd better keep finding things to keep us busy."

He turned the plane and headed in the other direction. "Let's start with flying over those houses on the lake — we need to make that decision together."

He gave her the signature half-smile and a wink. "Shall we see what the one with the beach that you liked so much looks like from up here?"

Chapter 47

Rick was reading Rachel's book over a cup of coffee when Joe Callahan came through the door. "Hi Joe. You just missed Emily."

"I know. I was waiting down the street until she was gone because I wanted your help with a surprise. Do you have a minute?"

Rick set the book down. "Sure, how can I help?"

Joe's excitement was palpable. "I'm wondering if you have any meetings scheduled with her to talk about the treatment center over the next couple of days, or if you could make one. I need her distracted and away from my house. She's been helping me so much with the renovations that I don't have any time there alone and I need to be alone to set up my surprise."

"We're meeting at Faith's in an hour to talk about next steps for the center. How much time do you need?"

"Shelby is on standby to help me, so we shouldn't need more than an hour. I'll send you a text when I'm ready for her to be free."

Rick's curiosity got the better of him. "It's none of my business, but is this a proposal you're planning?"

Joe grinned from ear to ear. "It is. I've been thinking I needed to hold off for Lily's sake and it's been killing me. I didn't want to rush into anything and have it be too much for her, but last night when I was giving her a bath, she asked me out of the blue when Emily was going to live with us and be her mommy and give her baths. We never talked about it in front of her and she just came out with it, so I decided to take that as a sign."

Rick smiled. "Sounds like a sign to me."

"I knew I was ready to marry Emily at Christmas, but thought I needed to wait. Now that Lily has unknowingly given me permission, I don't want to wait. I want Lily to have a mommy and I want Emily to be my wife as soon as possible." He gestured out the window. "The snow is too deep to get down on one knee on the beach where I first saw her. and my living room is the place where we had our first real conversation and started to get to know each other, so it seems fitting to propose there."

Rick smiled. "Congratulations, Joe. Emily is great and if I didn't know better and saw them together, I would have thought that she *was* Lily's mom. I've been in the same boat with Faith. We both know where this thing is going, but I've got this voice in my head saying I need to take it slow even though everything in me wants to move forward and ask her today."

Joe gave him a knowing look. "What do you need to know about her to know she's the right one?"

Now Rick was the one grinning.

"Not a thing. I've known she was the only one for me for twenty-six years. I've been trying to hold off because of my daughter too, but she doesn't need me to do that any more than yours does."

Joe shook his hand. "Congratulations to you, too. I'm sure Rachel is going to be as happy as you are. I guess we're set, then — I'll race you to the altar."

Chapter 48

Faith couldn't keep the smile from her face as she put the files away. She, Rick, Emily, and Pastor Ray had spent time praying for the center and putting the final touches on the paperwork they needed to file as a nonprofit with the state. Once Pastor Ray had agreed to serve on the board, they had the minimum number required and could start filing paperwork.

Rick seemed extra excited, too, and Faith loved being able to share the creation of the center with him. After ushering the others to the door, he came up behind her and put his arms around her waist as she put the papers away.

She felt the usual rush at his touch and leaned into him as she covered his hands with hers. "Rick, thank you for being a part of this with me. It's exciting to get this going, but it's even better with you here."

"I love being a part of it, too. Let's go celebrate with a cup of coffee on the bluff. I know we were hoping to get up in the plane again today, but with all this snow flying, we won't be able to see much. We'll have to save that ride for after I get back."

He was quiet on the short drive to the bluff and Faith basked in the comfort of being with him. She never thought she would see him again, and once he came back into Rachel's life she never thought she would want to spend a minute more with him than was absolutely necessary.

Now she couldn't get enough time with him. She was glad that he had extended his time in Hideaway for a few days before he returned to work, and she was trying not to think about the fact that he was leaving the next morning for five days.

When they reached the top of the bluff, he looked out at the snow falling over the water for a moment as if he was contemplating something, then turned to her and took her hand. "Do you realize that most of the pivotal conversations we've had since we've been back in each other's lives have taken place in this car and most have taken place in this spot?"

She smiled. "That's true. This is a good car for conversations and confessions." She chuckled as she added, "and even fights."

He laughed, but then turned serious.

"I'm so thankful we had that fight in this car. Who knows how long it would have taken us to find out the truth — and to *believe* the truth about each other — if we hadn't been so mad and laid it all out there. Plus, I always liked fighting with you because you never backed down."

He grinned and she did too as she remembered some of the fighting and making up they'd done in college.

She kissed his hand. "We've always been pretty good at that, haven't we? I'm glad we're even better at making up and making things right. I'm glad we took the time to make things right between us, and look at what we've done in the last few weeks. We've gotten back together, we've formed a family around our daughter, and we're forming a business that will help other families. We're a good team."

"We're a *great* team, Faith."

He reached across and pulled her near as he looked intently into her eyes.

"I've been trying to keep the brakes on, but I can't. I love you and I want to spend the rest of my life making up for all the time we've missed." She couldn't blink for fear of missing something as he spoke. "I don't even want to lose time by waiting for the weather to cooperate for the romantic way I wanted to propose to you. Will you please just marry me as soon as possible so we can get on with our life together?"

She threw her arms around him. "Yes! As soon as possible."

It took everything in her to stop herself from kissing him like she wanted to. She told herself that they could wait for that, but he turned his face toward her and kissed her with a passion that she had never experienced, even with him.

He pulled back and he looked like he was going to say something, but Faith put her finger over his lips.

"Don't you dare apologize for that kiss, Rick Weston."

They both laughed and drew together again for more. When he pulled back again, they were both as out of breath as if they had just climbed the hill they were parked on.

"What I was going to say, future Mrs. Weston, is that I've missed your kiss for twenty-six years — I've missed everything about you and can't wait to make you my wife." He planted another tiny, soft kiss on the corner of her mouth. "In the spirit of protecting your honor, I need to get us out of these close quarters. Let's go find out what it takes to get a marriage license around here and talk to Pastor Ray about arranging a wedding when I get back."

"Perfect."

She looked out over the bluff one last time. "Thank You, Lord. You sure are big."

As they drove off to the county clerk's office, she felt a peace and excitement she had been missing for twenty-six years and had more hope for the next twenty-six than she ever thought possible.

Dear Reader,

Hopefully if you've read this far, you enjoyed the book! I know you're busy and have other things (and books!) clamoring for your time and attention, and I hope this story brought a little brightness into your day.

I absolutely loved writing Rick and Faith's story and didn't want it to end. As with the other characters from the series, they will continue to show up in smaller roles in other books, including the next one. We haven't heard the last of the treatment center, either!

If you want to me the first to know about sales and new releases, come on over and join my mailing list at https://landing.mailerlite.com/webforms/landing/s3y2v2. I know, that's a clunky and big string to type in, but until we can point and click in a paperback book, this is the best I can do :) Some new Summit County goodies that will only be available to newsletter subscribers will be coming soon!

If you would like to leave a review on any of your favorite book sites so that other readers can be introduced to this book, I would be so grateful. In the meantime, keep reading!

See you in Summit County,

Katherine

Taking Risk in Summit County

When he looked across the room and saw the person he'd known for years in a whole new light, he knew she was off-limits and fought the feelings as hard as he had ever fought anything.

She had known he was off-limits for years and had moved on from the feelings she once had for him, or so she thought.

When their circumstances keep throwing them together, it gets harder and harder to hold on to the reasons they each have for staying away from each other. They had each learned from painful experience that life didn't go along with their carefully concocted plans, and when they stop fighting against their desires, the real fight begins as they decide what to do with life's uncertainty.

Available in paperback and Kindle on Amazon!

About the Author

Katherine Karrol is both a fan and an author of sweet, clean Christian romance stories. Because she does not possess the ability or desire to put a good book down and generally reads them in one sitting, she writes books that can be read in the same way.

Her books are meant to entertain, encourage, and even possibly inspire the reader to take chances, trust God, and laugh at life as much as possible. The people she interacts with in her professional life have absolutely no idea that she writes these books, so by reading this, you agree to keep her secret.

If you would like to contact her to share your favorite character or share who you were picturing as you were reading, you can follow her on Goodreads, Facebook, Twitter, and Instagram, or email her at KatherineKarrol@gmail.com.

Books in the Summit County Series

Made in the USA
Monee, IL
23 September 2020